Damaged

Initiation into Submission: High Protocol

By

KyAnn Waters

This is a work of fiction. Names, characters, places, and incidents are either the product of the author's imagination or are used fictitiously, and any resemblance to actual persons living or dead, business establishments, events, or locales, is entirely coincidental.

Contact Information: kyannwaters@hotmail.com

Visit www.KyAnnWaters.com

Chapter One

I'm damaged.

Saying those words should have cut like a knife slicing through her. But they didn't. Evelyn Larsen hadn't felt normal...not since she'd lost Daniel.

"I'm worried about you. Your family is worried." Misty Kemp, her best friend since third grade, unloaded groceries onto her counter.

Her family was in mourning...for her. They worried about the woman she'd been, and they worried about the woman she'd become. She heard their whispers of concern like a gossamer veil surrounding her. She couldn't explain to them that their words and worry wouldn't help. "You don't need to do this. I can get my own groceries."

"I know." Misty crossed to the table and sat next to Evelyn. Misty wore jeans and a bright blue T-shirt with a succubus and the words *I Don't Need to Flirt* scrawled across the front. "I know you don't want to deal with whatever is going on inside your head. I can't imagine how you're hurting. I'm so sorry." She covered Evelyn's hand with her own. "Come out with me and the guys from work. We're going to Roosters. Evie, you can't live in your memories of Daniel."

Evelyn pulled her hand back. Memories. She could remember when the late summer sun had been warm on her face. She and Daniel had taken a trip to the coast. Sea and citrus scents had drifted on the salty air. If she closed her eyes and held perfectly still, she could almost remember the feel of Daniel's lips pressed to hers, the slide of his tongue as he sipped from her mouth. Before she could fully grasp the memory, it slipped from her mind just as the warm white sand had slipped through her fingers.

"All I have are memories." She remembered their passion. A simple glance from Daniel could weaken her knees. Loving him, sex with him, was all she'd needed.

"It's been a year, Evie. I know you don't want to hear this, but at some point, you have to let him go. We all loved Daniel. We all miss him. It's okay to cry."

"I know." But lately, the tears wouldn't come. Sometimes, Evelyn wondered what was wrong with her. She wanted to drown in her emotions. Really, she did. She ached to sink beneath the dark rippling waters of regret. The doctors called it survivor's guilt. "My mother told me to get on a dating app." A smile curled her lips. "I told her I wasn't looking for sex."

Misty laughed. "You should be. Come to Roosters." She wagged her brows. "It's full of cocks."

Evelyn laughed with a snort.

Misty sighed. "She doesn't want to see you alone. You need to get out, live again, and maybe you will fall in love again."

Love again? Love was a strong word. She remembered the day she'd become his, the perfect words he whispered and the weight of his ring on her finger.

Misty stood. "He wouldn't want to see you this way. The woman he loved was adventurous and fun. He wouldn't have wanted to see you hurting...and to know he was the cause. He'd want you to remember the good times."

The memories didn't bring her comfort. Just like they didn't hurt. *I don't feel anything. So I must be dead, too.*

"I have to get back to work. That bitch Rebecca called in again today. I swear she's either screwing my boss, Walt, or she's screwing someone else upstairs, because there's no way the rest of us would get away with the shit she does. Cary's covering for me."

"You talk a lot about him."

"Absolutely not like that. But he'll be at Roosters. You might like him." She paused at the door. "It'll be fun. Have a couple drinks. Dance. Laugh. Live. Do you want to come? I think your sister is coming, too."

"Then it's a definite no." She shrugged. "I'm going to be working."

She would work. Every day was the same. She still woke every morning and went to bed alone every night. Another week went by. Another month. Another eighty-four days. Another two thousand and sixteen hours... She could go on but understood time was relative when one simply existed. She'd rather one day blended into the next. Now that she'd lost her job as a paralegal, lost her lover, and lost herself, what was the point of trying to pull herself together?

"Call me if you change your mind."

She wouldn't. Wouldn't call or change her mind. If Evelyn knew someone like herself, she'd tell them they were pathetic. Life went on. But she couldn't stand the thought of pretending. Pretending to care about anyone else. Pretending to move on. She recognized she wasn't a pleasant person...not anymore. Even if she could feel again, it wouldn't have to be happiness.

Evelyn finished putting away the groceries, and then started a pot of dark roast. At least she'd showered today, pulled her hair into a ponytail. With a cup of coffee in hand, she sat at the computer to work on her latest assignment.

After losing her job, she started working freelance, doing research for an online resource. It didn't require her to think, just browse websites and compile information and document her sources. This time the project was an online resource for people interested in alternative lifestyles. Kink, BDSM, swinging — the basic smorgasbord of hedonism for those whose only intrinsic pursuit was pleasure.

She supposed one didn't open the yellow pages looking for those specializing in fetishes to get off. In her research, she'd found blogs, forums, and groups. After checking social media, searching on keywords with a few search engines, she found there were a number of twisted people looking for something to make them complete.

A few clicks, and she scanned the webpage on the monitor. What made people do this? The woman on the screen knelt on a slate gray dungeon floor. Weapons of the pleasuring sort hung on a pegboard wall behind her. Three men clad in leather pants, not all that attractive, circled her.

But it was the wording to the side that drew her interest. The woman belonged to all three men. They'd given her the name Patience. The article stated Patience had agreed to a Total Power Exchange. Twenty-four hours a day, seven days a week, she lived to serve them. The collar with D-rings strapped around her neck represented their claim on her.

Evelyn had been Daniel's, but not the way these men cared for Patience. She was owned, never having to feel for herself. Responsibility for her rested with these three. In a small way, Evelyn envied the woman.

Another page showed a petite woman with her hands tied behind her back. Much of her body was bound with rope. The side of the picture described Japanese Kinbaku. A series of intricate knots moored her arms to her sides. Coiled rope wound her breasts, leaving her bound, darkened nipples exposed.

Evelyn made notes for the assignment, copied the website URL, and then clicked on another page, but her mind couldn't stop the disturbing images from playing in continuous morbid curiosity. She wanted to know more.

Her breath caught. A beautiful blonde woman with long wavy hair had her arms stretched above her head and her legs spread, anchored to the base of a Saint Andrew's Cross. There appeared to be an altar of sorts to her left. Red candles burned, and gold brocade draped the front. What must the woman's sins be to deserve crucifixion?

With a few keystrokes, she discovered it wasn't a religious ritual. Her pleasure came from total submission. Angel, as the article named her, lived a full Master and slave lifestyle. She was his property — to love or to let go when he was done with her so she could serve another.

Evelyn's stomach fluttered, and heat simmered low in her belly, warming her. Her heartbeat spiked. Sweat broke along her brow. She snapped off the monitor and scrambled away from the computer. Covering her mouth with her trembling fingers, she closed her eyes and took a few deep breaths. But her heart continued to race.

Behind her closed eyes, she continued to see the woman on the computer. Her lips slightly parted, her focus on the man standing next to her. His chest toned, muscles in her arms flexed as he held a leather wand with tassels. Evelyn knew what he would do to the slave. The blush of crimson stained her thighs and shoulders, evidence of the strikes to her smooth flesh.

Moisture flooded Evelyn's panties. Alarm streaked through her, worry for the woman who would want to submit, and for the man who needed dominance over her. Horror mixed with arousal. Her lips quivered.

For the first time since Daniel died, Evelyn felt again.

She felt fear.

Chapter Two

Alex Ferraro sat in the back of the black limo. In any other city, he wouldn't use a service, but he'd taken his private jet to San Francisco to finish the negotiations on a building in the Financial District. For the past couple of months, he'd been in the market for a new location for his west coast headquarters. He'd always enjoyed San Francisco, and this would give him an excuse to spend more time in his Pacific Heights loft.

He tapped the button for speakerphone and called Nash.

"Are you in town?" Nash asked without a hello.

"Just landed and I'm on my way to the loft. Are we set for three this afternoon? Because I don't want to be stuck in traffic. I want to get in and get out." He sighed. "I have a feeling this is going to be a waste of time."

Nash Corbett had been by his side since their days at Harvard. They'd discovered early on their parallel interests and proclivities toward edgier forms of entertainment. Five years ago, Nash had settled down, married his sub, Nadia, and now had a three-year-old little girl named Ava. Once she arrived, Nash stopped being the Master of his own home.

"The property has been on the market for six months," Nash said.

That meant overpriced, structural issues, regulation and code enforcement, or location problems. None of which he wanted to deal with. While still beautiful, the city wasn't without her issues. Alex leaned back in the seat and pinched the bridge of his nose.

"I think Frank is overpriced for the location." Nash gave him his assessment.

"Frank Dunn?"

"You remember him?"

Alex groaned. The guy was an ass. Rumors swirled that he'd made some bad investments and now had to liquidate. "I've heard he's in trouble. He passed on offers early on, and now the market has slowed. He knows you're a cash buyer."

"No games. I'm not in the mood. He takes our offer, or he can fuck off."

"I'm sure he knows. You're the boss. He's met you before."

"Give me an hour." Alex loosened his tie. "I'm going to the loft first." For whatever reason, and he didn't care why, he couldn't shake his negative attitude. Generally, he enjoyed his time in the city...especially time spent at Salvage, a dungeon in the North Beach area.

"I'll meet you there."

"At Salvage?"

Nash laughed. "I don't need to ask where your head is at. I thought I'd meet you at the loft and we could ride over to the building together. But I'm not opposed to your suggestion."

"What about Nadia?" Alex wasn't privy to the details of their marital arrangement, and he didn't care to know.

"As long as I remember her rules, she's fine with it." Nash chuckled. "She has some project she's doing with her girlfriends."

"You don't mind her going out without you?"

"More of a don't ask, don't tell policy for us. If I know, I might have to be involved. And if I'm involved…"

"Right. I get it." Alex didn't allow anyone to make decisions for him. Nash was the same way.

If Alex went to the club…rather *when* he went to the club, he didn't want distractions. "What about Ava?"

"That's what the nanny is here for."

"See you in an hour."

Alex hadn't been to the loft in a couple months. He had a cleaning service that kept the two bedroom, fifteen-hundred square foot apartment tidy. He pressed the numbers to the keyless entry. The mechanical locks turned. With his computer case over his shoulder, he pushed open the door. A mirror, edged in chrome stretched the length of the long corridor leading to the main room of the loft.

God, he looked like shit. He combed his fingers through his hair as he strode toward the bank of windows overlooking the bay. He left his computer case on the white leather sofa and went to the master suite. The second bedroom masqueraded as an office.

He stripped out of his shirt as he made his way into the open bathroom. By the time they finished with their meeting, talked business, and grabbed some dinner, he'd be ready for the club.

Alex finished undressing and stepped into the glass enclosed shower. Hot water cascaded over him from multiple showerheads. He closed his eyes, ran his hand over his torso until he reached his cock. Curling his fingers around the base, he enjoyed the hardening of the shaft as he slowly stroked from groin to tip.

This is what his sex life had become. Masturbating in the shower. Fucking subs in the dungeon wasn't doing much for him. He loved the play, the power exchange, and the responsibility of getting his partner off. But lately, at the end of the night, he'd have had an orgasm, *sometimes*, but he hadn't relieved a simmering need for more than a quick release. He could come with his fist, like he did now. Muscles tensed. He squeezed hard, his balls tightened, and he shot his load into the spray of hot water.

Pressure from pent-up energy had eased, but he wasn't spent. He wanted to be milked dry and sore from a night of fucking. He wanted his sub delirious with pleasure. But he didn't want the complication of a commitment. Not even a contracted commitment.

"Boss?"

Alex turned off the water and wrapped a

towel around his waist. "In here. Give me ten minutes." He quickly dried and scrubbed the towel over his hair.

"You don't have shit to eat in here," Nash said.

What the hell?

"My flight landed an hour ago." Alex had literally only had time to beat off in the shower. Negotiations with Frank would be more productive if he wasn't wound so tight. He at least wouldn't tell him to fuck off to his face but would let Nash handle it in a calmer, more professional way. "Call a delivery service. They have apps for it."

Alex opened the closet and grabbed a pair of faded jeans and a black turtleneck. He grabbed boots out of the bottom of the closet and a pair of socks from the drawer.

After he dressed, he strode to the kitchen. "I thought we could get a bite to eat after looking at the building and then head over to Salvage."

Nash sat on the leather sofa, his right ankle resting on his left knee. He scrolled through content on his phone. "Sounds good," he said without looking up.

The large open space of the loft was comprised of a living room, dining room, and kitchen. The aged brick walls complimented the modern stainless-steel appliances and tropical ebony cabinetry. However, the house was sterile and unappealing with white leather furniture and glass tables and shelving. Next time, he wouldn't let an eager-to-please sub with a degree in interior design decorate one of his homes.

Alex slipped on his sunglasses and stuffed his wallet into his pocket with his phone. "You can tell me more about the property on our way."

Nash stood and crossed the room. "I need Nadia to come see this place. Ava has remodeled our living room into a toy room." He put on his sunglasses and chuckled. "And no, not the kind of toys you're used to having around." He sighed. "Damn, but there are some things I miss."

They took the elevator down. "So you and Nadia don't play anymore?"

Nash shook his head. "Dude, Ava sleeps in our bed. I had to get rid of the straps, bindings, ropes. I had to buy a locking bureau for my equipment. The key never comes out. How would I explain to her that mommy needs a spanking?"

Alex paused and rested his hand on Nash's arm. "Do you regret it...the marriage, fidelity, settling?" He couldn't ask him if he regretted fatherhood. Alex knew the answer to that. His world revolved around Ava.

Nash smiled. "I haven't settled for anything. Life is great. Nadia is great. I told her you were in town. She wants you to come by for dinner."

"No time."

"That's what I told her." His lopsided smile curved his lips. "She called bullshit on that one. She said if you have time for Salvage, you have time for her."

"I'm taking the jet home in the morning." At the end of the day, he preferred his dungeon, High Protocol. While he liked a high stakes game in business and in the bedroom, he also liked his rules and his games in his playground.

The driver opened the door. Nash climbed in first, and Alex followed.

As they drove through the city, Nash updated him on the property. "Mixed use."

Nash understood Alex's business model. While he owned a lot of real estate, he'd also purchased buildings, businesses, and investments that could be subdivided and resold at a profit. He didn't make friends, unless they were on his side of the negotiating table, and then he made them millions.

Nash kept him out of sticky situations. Nash also had the unfortunate responsibility of keeping him from losing money.

"What about the leases?" Leases led to lawsuits.

"Unavoidable, but not long term. Won't be an issue."

Nash set the papers aside. "If you want the building, don't pay over sixty million for it. Any more and you'll cut into your ROI. I know how you feel about your return on your investments."

Nash knew him well. Better than most. And he was right. In every aspect of his life, the payoff had to be worth the work...the risk worth the reward.

Chapter Three

Evelyn had an ongoing conversation in her mind. For the past year, she'd made every excuse to stay locked inside her home. But another type of confinement held her thoughts hostage.

The computer wasn't enough. Never considering herself obsessive, Evelyn had become an addict searching for salvation. The shiver of fear had become a drug. After she'd felt the first rush, she found herself insatiable. She sought out more, intimate details into the dark dangerous world of BDSM. She learned about sexual slavery, mastering and submitting. With every morsel of depravity she consumed, her need grew.

Trepidation flooded through her thoughts. As sure as she knew she needed air to breathe, she believed this could be a way for her to live again. To feel again. She wanted a Master to dominate her. She wanted to be afraid, and she wanted to hurt.

But she also needed to pacify her family. That meant calling her mom back. The last thing she wanted was a police officer at the door for a welfare check.

When she picked up her cell, she stared at the screen. She still had a picture of her and Daniel's toes in the sand as her screen shot. Holding up the camera, she took a picture of the plain beige wall, tapped a few buttons, and changed the background on her phone. One less reminder of what she'd never have again.

She took a deep breath, pulled up her favorites, and slid her thumb across her mother's name. How long would it take to convince her mom that she was fine?

Mom answered on the first ring. "Honey, how are you?"

"Good. Just busy." Not really, but if she made it sound good, maybe she'd get another week or two of isolation.

"Dad is watching car racing. Why don't you come over and help me make dinner? Jane is coming over to work on the wedding plans. She needs your help." Her mother sighed. "And it would be good for you."

Helping her sister plan her wedding wouldn't be good for her. It wouldn't miraculously make her life worth more. "I think I'm just going to stay in."

"Evelyn, this isn't normal. People who are tired all the time, stay in their house, and refuse to be with family and friends…those people have depression. I was talking to Margaret about you."

"Mom, please don't talk about me with your neighbors."

"She's been my friend for thirty years and has known you her whole life. She knows about these things."

"No, Mom, she just thinks she knows

everything."

"Sweetie, I just want you to be happy. We all understand it's difficult."

Difficult. Taking the BAR exam would be difficult, digging a trench would be difficult, burying Daniel was difficult. Living with out him wasn't difficult. She wasn't living.

But she couldn't tell her mother that. She couldn't make her worry. Because she wasn't suicidal. She just accepted this was her life now. "Next weekend, Mom."

"Promise?"

No, she couldn't do that. Promises were made to be broken. She didn't trust promises. "I'll try."

For a moment after they hung up, she let her mom's worries and words seep into her. Then, called back to her dark obsession, her fingers danced across the keyboard as she searched for more dangerous games to play. She read blogs, searched out images, and imagined herself restricted, controlled, and forced to obey.

She stared at the page on the computer screen. Outside, city traffic blended with the rustle of wind against her windows. Nervous energy surged through her.

Her phone rang, and she jumped.

"Hi," she said to Misty, but her focus remained on the computer monitor.

What was she doing, contacting a group, a private community of individuals looking for a lifestyle outside of society's norms? She could attend a munch where she could meet those in the lifestyle outside a club or party. But she didn't want friends. She just wanted to be Patience, even if only for a moment.

Evelyn didn't even know if she'd be accepted for membership to a private dungeon. What sort of vetting would they do for membership?

"What are you up to?" Misty asked.

Her attention returned to the phone call. "Nothing much. Um...working on the computer." With trembling fingers, she sent an email, followed by a questionnaire. She stared at the confirmation screen. Butterflies swirled in her belly.

"Do you have plans today?" Misty asked.

Not yet, but maybe soon. "I thought I'd go shopping. Do you want to go with me?"

Misty squealed. "Hell, yes." Then she was quiet for the couple of seconds. "Not grocery shopping, right. A mall? Or the galleria?"

"No groceries." She didn't have much of an appetite. "I'll pick you up in thirty minutes."

If she stayed home, she'd sit in front of the computer, checking email every two minutes as she waited for a response. Instead, perhaps she could find something dark and dangerous to wear to a dungeon.

***

The mall was crowded. Saturday

afternoon. Teenagers gathered in small groups, and a high school band played in the common area, raising money for their upcoming season.

Misty pointed to the lingerie store. "Do you want to go in?"

They were having a sale. Evelyn followed Misty into the bra and panty section, but as Misty chatted with the sales associate about trying on the blue lace bra, Evelyn wandered into the rear of the store. Behind a partition, the store carried sex creams, toys, condoms, and other novelties.

Glancing over her shoulder, she assured she was alone. One wall had leather whips, fur-lined cuffs, anal plugs, and nipple clamps. Heat rushed through her, settling in her nipples. Her breath grew shallow. She imagined the pain of those steel teeth biting into her hardened nipples.

"You ready?"

She spun on her heels. "You scared me."

Misty approached. "Oh, my." She lifted a thick, long dildo from the wall. "This is what you need."

Evelyn wasn't interested in the dildo, but the whips, clamps and restraints… She was afraid Misty might be right.

They grabbed a bite to eat, then Evelyn's anxiety about the club forced her to call it a day. After dropping off Misty, she headed home.

How long did a BDSM dungeon need to vet their potential clients? How would they even be sure she was who she said she was? She'd given them her address, name, phone number, age, a photo, and written a paragraph about herself. She hadn't been completely honest about that part. She didn't really know who she was anymore.

Another freelance project hit her virtual desk.

"I am pathetic," she said to her monitor.

She made a deal with herself. She could research five sources before opening a new window in her browser and spending fifteen minutes in the online D/s chatroom she'd found. She rarely typed in the chat. She just lurked in the open forum, reading the titillating tales with rapt interest.

The ring of her smart phone sounded from an unknown number. Normally, she wouldn't answer, but she wasn't following her normal routine.

The deep sultry voice spoke her name. "Evelyn Larson?"

"Yes."

"My name is Ronan. Alex Ferraro has invited you to High Protocol."

Her breath caught. High Protocol, the BDSM dungeon where she'd submitted the questionnaire. They didn't just offer private rooms, experienced play, but they also mentioned private instruction.

"Tomorrow at eleven."

"In the morning?" She'd hoped this would

be more clandestine.

His soft chuckle vibrated through the phone, letting her know she'd been mistaken. He gave her the address and let her know the information was confidential per the agreement done through email. She remembered the clause on the questionnaire with the legalese. There was no mistaking the threat and consequences of disclosure. These were terms she understood, words that had been her passion...before she lost everything.

She agreed to be there and then realized she had no idea what to expect at a BDSM dungeon outside of what she'd learned online. The women in the pictures wore little to no clothing. Did they expect her to be naked? Of course, they would. But she wasn't interested in sex. She understood they intended to give her pleasure. She could endure that if it meant she could receive the punishment. If she could feel the bite of pain on her nipples, the burn of a flogger on her buttocks...give someone else the power to make her feel.

She just didn't want to be Daniel's Evelyn anymore.

Chapter Four

Evelyn showered and carefully styled her hair and applied her makeup. Her intent was to be appealing but not eager. Preparing for any eventuality, for the first time since Daniel died, she'd shaved more than her legs and underarms. The thought of having sex terrified her. She held on to the fear.

A niggle of guilt wormed into her belly, as if she were cheating on Daniel. But this wasn't cheating. This was moving on, and wasn't that what everyone had been trying to get her to do?

She grabbed her car keys and her small clutch and left the house. Anyone seeing her now would assume she was going on a date.

Did she wear the right clothing? A simple black skirt, and button-down blouse hid a lace bra and panties. She couldn't imagine wearing leather or, worse, nothing at all. Did she even want to be nude? A lack of attire didn't scare her. That the Master would take more than she was ready to give was what sent a frisson of disquiet through her tumbling thoughts. How far would she let them go? Everything she'd read led her to believe her Dom would know what she needed.

At the scheduled hour, she stumbled as she walked to the heavy wooden doors of High Protocol. She pressed the button and waited.

When prompted, she gave her name.

Thoughts flowed through her mind at warp speed. Her imagination had her selecting tortures as if she were ordering off a menu at a Chinese restaurant. Spankings, flogging, or would she prefer a whipping to go along with her rope and wax burns? Would she agree to sex? No. But fearing she might sent shivers, like a million prickles, over her flesh.

The door opened, and swallowing her insecurity, she took another step toward the unknown world she'd glimpsed through the filter of the internet.

Muted by the thick cinderblock walls, a heavy beat thrummed through her chest. Standing in the foyer, she felt as if she couldn't catch her breath. Sensations Evelyn had nearly forgotten surged through her. Tightness, like a python forcing the air from her lungs, gripped her chest. A hive of wasps swarmed her stomach.

One shiny black door was blocked by a security guard. Muscles bulged beneath the tight black T-shirt. Black jeans hugged his hips, molded to the mound of his crotch, and stretched across his muscular thighs. He wasn't smiling, but the tilt of his lips wasn't a scowl either, more of an unreadable expression. Intimidating, like the men she expected to meet in the club. Perhaps he was a Dom. Not the type of Master that Evelyn needed though. She didn't want powered over with brute force, but rather quiet strength. A man who could make her tremble with a whisper.

"Alex Ferraro?"

The security guard pointed to a door on the left.

"Thank you," she said. The door clicked as it unlocked. The steel was cool under her heated fingertips. With a slow turn of the handle, she entered.

The room wasn't as she expected. Instead of dark, seedy, mysterious, and just a little dirty, abstract art in polished chrome frames hung on walls painted taupe. Plush gray carpet with flecks of silver covered the floor and stretched into the glass-walled office in the distance.

Research hadn't prepared her for this reality. A man, whom she could only assume was the man she had to see in order to gain access to the club, sat behind his desk, a phone to his ear. His gaze lifted.

A jolt of awareness flared through her. Unlike the security guard in the foyer, this man radiated an aura of authority that saturated the room, touching her in every way. Dark brows arched over darker piercing eyes fringed with black lashes. A shadow of a beard covered his angular jaw. He set the phone on his desk and then stood. As he stepped around the desk, he smiled. A dimple creased his left cheek.

"Hello, Evelyn." He said her name as if he'd whispered it a thousand times and knew what it could do to her. "Please, come in." She was expected after all.

Long, strong fingers curled around her hand. He held it a moment longer than friendly. As if unable to resist the magnetic pull, she entered his lair. Tightness clenched her chest as a hum tingled through her hardened nipples. Warmth pooled in her core. Dangerous sensations because she knew what he was. Unlike the men on the internet, this man exuded confidence and power with the slight tilt of his lips, the upper slightly fuller than the lower.

Erotic awareness stole over her as his gaze roamed her figure. Would this man bind a woman's hands behind her back, blindfold her, lash her with the feathering tails of a crop before he unlocked her secrets? She wanted those forbidden feelings, emotions, and sensations. She desperately needed to be taken to the place she'd only read about. Subspace.

"Evelyn." He said her name again, with more passion, drawing her eyes to his.

"Yes. Alex Ferraro?"

"Yes." His smile widened, and his dimple deepened. "I'm glad you're here."

Sitting in the chair he offered, she stated, "I'm not sure how I feel about being here, but…" How did she tell him that it wasn't about wanting this but needing? If she had to say the right answers, she shouldn't say too much.

He took his seat behind the desk. "You don't have to be sure? And it's okay to change your mind."

"No, it's not that. I'm sure I want to be here." She'd seen enough online to know she had to be here. She also understood enough of the rules to know that, even now, his knowing gaze was trying to see into her. He wanted her secrets. She just wanted his power. "I won't change my mind."

He leaned back in his chair. "You spoke with Ronan on the phone, and I received your profile."

She'd filled out questionnaires, defined hard and soft limits. Now, that file lay on his desk. In the answers, she'd sworn complete honesty. Would he know she lied?

"You're here because you've looked through the window, but that doesn't mean this will feel like home."

No, she didn't want it to feel like home. Home was where time stood still. But he didn't need to know the reasons, only that she wanted to experience what his dungeon offered. "I'm sure."

His stare focused hard on her. Then he placed his hand on the smooth polished surface of his desk and slid over the file. "I'm glad." He opened the folder. "Evelyn, this is your contract. Safe. Sane. Consensual. This is probationary, a trial."

Could he see her fingers, how they trembled as he handed over a pen from the stationary on his desk? Their fingers brushed.

Tamping down the surge of emotions, she concentrated on the words on the paper. Not only was she sworn to confidentiality, but her dark secrets were plainly written out. She didn't want to bleed, didn't want to submit in front of anyone but the man who would be her Master for the session. She didn't want to be on display in the playrooms. And even though she had to choose one, she didn't want to use a safeword. But part of her, the part that felt afraid, needed to know the risks were there. She needed to be pushed into submission. She wanted to be afraid to say no.

After scrawling her name across the bottom of the page, she set the pen on the table, the soft click loud in the quiet room. Anticipation morphed into anxiety. "What now?"

Alex leaned forward, the leather chair creaking under his imposing height and stature. "Let's talk about your Dom. You reserved a training session, an introduction."

Her heart took a little jolt just hearing that she would have a Dom, a man to master her emotions. How did she choose? Was it an interview where one selected the best candidate for the job?

"The most important part of a D/s relationship is trust." A gentle smile curled his lips. "Trust isn't easy for anyone."

She hadn't thought about trust. "I suppose I'm putting my trust in you."

A muscle in his jaw ticked, and something in his gaze intensified. A shiver of awareness skittered over her flesh. If she hadn't been sure before, she was now. Alex Ferraro had to be a Dom. Envisioning him in a position of authority, she wasn't sure if she wanted someone so handsome, so sexually intense. She wanted to feel pain because she wasn't ready for pleasure. Perhaps he needed to know that.

"I trust you to set the scene and to find a Dom who can wield a whip." Just thinking of the sting of the tail slicing across her buttocks had her pulse racing. She folded her hands in her lap. She hadn't submitted yet. This might be her only chance to express her needs. "Alex," His name sounded strange on her lips. He cocked a brow, encouraging her to continue. "Perhaps we should discuss what I want from the scene."

He lifted her contract and slipped it back into the folder. "That is for your Dom to decide."

"But what if he wants to do more, more than I'm ready for?"

He paused, folding his hands on the desk. "Tell me your safeword."

She stared into his eyes. "Patience," she whispered. The name of the woman she saw online, the woman she wanted to be.

"Say it, and the scene stops."

She nodded.

***

What the fuck was wrong with him? His

dick was hard, his palms damp, and his heart hammered in his chest. Until she'd walked into his office, Alex was sure he'd have her spinning on her heels and leaving the same way she came in. Rarely did he allow anyone into the club without a reference. He didn't take risks.

But he'd opened his email, read her promise of compliance, and been hooked on the desperation in her eyes. In her photo, a picture he could only guess she'd snapped of herself as she filled out the questionnaire, her naturally tawny brown hair hung to her shoulders in soft waves. She hadn't applied filters to the shot, hadn't worn more than a bit of mascara. However, now, sitting across from him, he wasn't sure. Her long lashes lowered as she glanced down at her hands folded in her lap.

Mentally, he shook his head. What was he doing? This was foolish, reckless, and for him, dangerous. He played in the club, enjoyed a scene, and had a handful of women he called his pets. She was too innocent and yet instinctively submissive. She would empower her Dom. He recognized a need in her, a need he couldn't fulfill because he didn't live the lifestyle. Not anymore and never again. He wasn't Nash. BDSM in the dungeon had to be enough to satisfy his needs.

But then he looked at Evelyn and those needs he'd buried deep bubbled to the surface. He didn't train subs. Which was why he was turning her over to Dario. "Are you ready?"

"Yes." She squared her shoulders, lifted her chin, and took a deep breath as she stood.

Damn. Trying to be brave. So unsure yet attempting to show strength. Taking her down, showing her the power in submission would be a gift...a gift for Dario.

Only Dario wouldn't see it that way. This would be nothing more than assignment. That made Dario perfect for Evelyn. She would cling quickly, grow needy as she accepted her submission. Power was intoxicating. Dario loved training, but once the power exchange was complete, the training over, so was his reason for involvement. Other Doms wanted perfectly trained pets. That was why Dario was known as the Professor.

"Are you going to teach me?"

"No, I prefer experienced subs." Because, for him, training required an emotional investment. He'd done that once. Nash understood him best. Alex had to consider his return on an investment and if the risk would be worth the reward.

Alex escorted her from his office. He nodded to Joel, the bouncer at the door, and took Evelyn through his private entrance to the club. Like a shot of liquid adrenaline, taking her into his lair had his heart racing, his cock kicking, and his resolve faltering.

"How long does it take one to become experienced?"

The question punched him in the gut. "Depends on the sub." And depended just as much on the Dom. "Experience doesn't mean a partnership stops evolving." Exploring new limits and new scenes continued to strengthen a bond in a D/s relationship, even if the relationship existed exclusively within the club setting.

"Through here." He opened a heavy polished black door with the word private embossed in gold across the front.

She paused hesitant to enter. "It's dark."

"Trust me." He rested his palm on her lower back and ushered her into the room. Heat from her body seeped into his hand, warmed his blood, and sent a rush of awareness into his groin. "Your eyes will adjust."

Most subs in training were hesitant to be in bright lights. Preset notions of what they wanted and needed being wrong or taboo had to be overcome.

She nodded and slowly entered. Once in the center of the room, she spun in a slow circle taking in the details. A private dungeon. But one of comfort. This was a training room, one that Alex used to enjoy. But now, this was Dario's private playpen. Padded tools, fur-lined leather restraints and silk bindings to begin with. Later the St. Andrew's Cross, bite bars, and floggers.

"This is where your first session will be. The Professor will be your Master. He's unbending and firm. He expects obedience." He softened his voice. "And he'll punish you when you aren't." He touched her, letting his fingertips trail across the soft curve of her biceps. "But during training, he's gentle."

She spun. "No."

Instinct had him reaching for her, curling his fingers over her shoulders, and holding her. "This is what you requested. What you said you wanted." She'd been specific. Evelyn wanted punished into submission.

"I do, but I don't want him to be gentle."

"BDSM—Doms and subs—isn't about pain...unless the pain reveals a deeper pleasure. Hurt not harm." Whatever was damaged inside her could be healed, to know she could endure discomfort, sometimes bordering on pain, to reach the pinnacle of pleasure.

"I know why I'm here."

"She's ready." The voice came from the corner.

She jumped, taking a step back and breaking contact between his fingers and the gentle slope of her shoulder.

Dario stepped forward. Muted light glinted off his shaved head. Alex recognized the spark of anticipation in his dark eyes and the clench of his jaw beneath his close-cut chin curtain.

Alex gritted his teeth and inhaled through his nose. He had to get out of the room. The predator in Dario had found his prey. This, Alex couldn't watch. Not with a woman like Evelyn. "Evelyn, I leave you in the capable hands of the Professor."

Her eyes widened as her gaze shifted between Alex and Dario. "Will I see you again?"

Yes. The pull to her was strong, but he was stronger. If anything, he knew how to master his own weaknesses. Weaknesses Evelyn could too easily expose. "Once the Professor finishes your training, you'll have access to the dungeon. I'll see you there."

"Once I'm experienced?"

Even then, she wouldn't be a sub for Alex. He turned and took two steps toward the door. "If you have questions, ask the Professor."

"I'll take it from here, Boss."

Once out of the room, Alex leaned against the wall and drew in a deep inhale. Regret like a knife twisted in his gut. He wanted to be the one to train her. Hypnotizing eyes to longingly stare into, smooth flesh to bloom under the stinging caress of his palm, and trembling words of adoration when she floated in the warm intoxicating haze of submission.

Unable to resist, he slipped through the unmarked door to the left. Dario's office. Not only was there a connecting door to his training lair, but a one-way mirror. As long as Alex remained in the darkened office, he'd be able to observe Evelyn's training.

He stood at the glass. Almost as if Dario

knew Alex was there, he turned Evelyn in his direction. She faced the mirror. Dario positioned behind her and whispered in her ear.

Alex pressed the intercom button to hear the exchange.

"Our relationship is built on trust. Do you trust me?"

She bit her bottom lip as she contemplated her answer. "I don't know you."

"You have no reason not to trust me."

She nodded. "I want to trust you." Her eyes slid closed. "But I'm not sure I trust myself."

"I understand. Remember, you have the power to end all of this." He closed the space between them, moving in closer. His lips brushed the shell of her ear. "I trust you to use your safeword."

She swallowed hard and nodded.

"Say it once."

She swallowed again.

"Evelyn, I need to hear it, so I know you'll remember it."

She closed her eyes. Her lips trembled as she whispered, "Patience."

"Good girl. Remove your skirt, Evie."

Her eyes snapped open. "I...I..."

"Tonight, you can speak freely. But only for tonight. If there is something that needs said, you should say it now. Or the next word I want to hear from your lips is Patience."

"Please, don't call me Evie. Not here."

"Why?" Dario waited for her answer.

"Because I don't want to be Evie anymore, especially not here."

Alex ached to hold her, to tell her that her past wouldn't matter, not in a dungeon. High Protocol was his safespace. And it could be hers, too. If she trusted Dario enough to let him in.

"Evelyn, remove your skirt."

Was she testing her safeword in her mind? Because she didn't speak it and she didn't obey the command. Her movements were slow, hesitant.

"I won't ask you again. You said you understood the rules."

"But you said we wouldn't have sex, so why do I need to undress?"

Dario kissed her temple. "Because I told you to."

Accepting the simple answer, she slid the side zipper down. The skirt slipped from her hips and pooled at her feet. A tiny scrap of pink satin covered her smooth sex. Heat surged through Alex, intensifying in his groin. She was beautiful, and he shouldn't be watching. This wasn't his scene, she wasn't his sub, and she never would be.

Dario's fingers deftly slipped the buttons of her blouse. Peeling the thin fabric from her shoulders, he slid the garment from her body.

Evelyn's head bowed, and her arms hung at her sides. Her small hands curled into fists.

From his position, Alex could see the rapid flutters of her chest as she breathed. She swallowed, seeming to struggle to hold still. He had been in the scene long enough to know that BDSM attracted diversity. Both men and women had their reasons. No one had the same story. He wanted to know hers.

He drank in the sight of her small, perfectly round breasts. Darkened nipples strained against the sheer lace bra. She was beautiful. Trim thighs, a sexy womanly curve to her belly. She was thin, not muscular, and not unhealthy. She was built like a woman with rounded hips, soft contours and smooth flesh. He breathed deeply wishing he could draw in her scent.

Dario crossed the room. Along with a wall of torturous tools of delight, he had drawers filled with clamps, dildos, ball gags, and any other item he desired. When he returned to Evelyn, he positioned in front of her. Alex shifted, uselessly trying to see around him.

Evelyn moaned. Alex stood and approached the mirror. He rested his palms on the glass, desperate to know what Dario was doing to her. Evelyn cried out again.

"You'll get used to them," Dario said.

"It hurts."

"It's supposed to. Do you like it?"

"Yes," she breathlessly whispered. Then she moaned again as her knees buckled.

Dario wrapped his arms around her. Alex tightened his hands into fists. Pain, but not for pleasure. Evelyn was only looking to be hurt. Dario had to show her the true meaning of submission. A Dom's power came from recognizing the gift of submission. Dario couldn't just hurt her because she wanted it. Evelyn didn't know that yet, but she'd learn. The woman wore armor against emotions. Alex could strip that away, but he wouldn't be able to remain unaffected.

Alex spun away from the window. This was the Professor. He knew what he was doing. Unable to resist, Alex turned back to the glass.

Evelyn knelt on the floor, her body braced against a padded bench. Dario had removed her bra, although she still wore the pink satin panties. Screw clamps pinched each of her reddened nipples. With lips slightly parted and eyes closed, she absorbed the strikes from Dario's paddle.

The burst of rose-hued flesh to her buttocks only made her more alluring. She wiggled, arching her back and bracing against the swats. Dario could've restrained her. Her responses were instinctual but against what she needed. Alex would have strapped her arms behind her back, braced her against the bench, and forced her immobility. The confinement would make her feel as if she had even less control. He'd also have opted for momentary sting of a braided tassel. But this wasn't his scene.

The Professor had his own techniques.

Dario knelt behind Evelyn and softly blew against her heated flesh. She shivered, whimpering. Sweat glistened on the feminine contours of her spine and shoulders. Her lower back dipped as her buttocks braced against the next whack of the paddle.

Dario faced the mirror and stared directly at Alex although he would only be seeing his own reflection in the mirror.

Turning away from the mirror, Dario stripped off his shirt. His torso, covered in tattoos, rippled with muscles. He squatted next to Evelyn and gently brushed damp tendrils of hair from her face. She lifted her head. Red rimmed eyes stared longingly at Dario. Tears streaked her cheeks, and teeth marks dented her trembling lower lip. But Alex didn't see the bliss of submission in her eyes. Rather the frustration of fighting it.

"Would you like a drink of water?" he quietly asked her.

"Yes," she croaked.

"Please address me as Professor."

She barely nodded, and her delicate pink tongue moistened her lips. "Yes, Professor."

Dario crossed the room. Taking a bottle of water from the small fridge, he twisted off the lid, poured it into a glass, and returned to Evelyn. She wrapped her hands over his and brought the edge of the glass to her lips. Her eyes slid closed as she took several swallows.

"Thank you, Professor."

Dario kissed her shoulder and slid his lips along her flesh to the curve of her neck.

She stiffened.

"Relax," Dario whispered. "There is more to learn than punishment." He helped her to sit on the bench, a bench that only a moment before had braced her chest. He stared into her eyes as he flicked his finger against her nipple.

Evelyn's lips pursed, and her shoulders hunched as if trying to retreat from the touch.

"I can tell you want to say something. I haven't forbidden you from speaking."

"I don't…"

"Don't what?"

"I don't need the intimacy. I don't need you to pretend to care for me."

Dario snapped the clamp from her nipple and quickly squeezed her nipple between his thumb and finger. She cried out.

He bent, closed his mouth over the red tip, and gently sucked. Evelyn's head fell back, her lips parted, and her thighs clamped together.

Dario laved the peak. "That isn't for you to decide. I don't expect you to understand everything I do, but I expect you to do as I say. It's the only way our relationship can progress."

"I didn't consider this a relationship."

A small smile curved his lips. "I assure you, I do, and you will." He removed the other clamp, bent down, and latched his mouth to the red, succulent tip of her perfect breast.

With a cry of pleasurable pain, Evelyn gripped his head, holding the Professor tight to her chest. She squeezed her eyes tightly closed, gently shaking her head no.

Alex wanted to rush in and rescue her from Dario. She endured, but she wasn't submitting. She mentally fought. Alex could see it in the stiffening of her shoulders, the tight clench of her fists, and the hard line of her reddened lips.

Dario shifted his mouth to the other breast, nipping at the peak with teeth and open mouth kisses.

Alex closed his eyes, imagining it was his mouth on her sweet nipple, her tender heated flesh in his hands as he gripped her buttocks. There was something so broken in her, something in her a Dom wanted to fix with his special type of persuasion. With the right instruction, would she become pliant and open? He wouldn't just want her submission. He'd want her soul.

His eyes snapped open. His mouth pulled into a tight line, and he watched Dario administer his after care. He better not attempt to fuck her. Alex could take anything but not that.

Raining gentle kisses over her face, her nose, and cheeks, finally, Dario kissed her eyes closed. Then he took her mouth. A slow thorough sweep of tongues and lips. Evelyn's hand clenched at her side, her other braced against

Dario's bare chest. Was she keeping him at a distance, or was she feeling his heat and power? Was there fight in her to push him away...or urge him closer?

That she kept her legs tightly closed didn't escape Alex's notice. Slowly, Dario pulled away from her. "That is your first lesson," he said.

"I...I can take more."

He softly kissed her lips. "That's enough for tonight." He tucked her hair behind her ear and smiled. "Don't question me. Get dressed. I expect you here tomorrow at nine."

"Tomorrow?"

He gathered her clothing and helped her to dress. "Yes. Tomorrow. Is there a problem?"

She bowed her head. "No, Professor. Tomorrow night at nine. I'll be here."

Chapter Five

Alex dragged his hands down his cheeks. What was wrong with him? Normally, putting on his favorite leather pants, black T-shirt, and black boots built a slow burn in his gut. By the time he entered the club for a scene, he'd be full of fire. The heady power of dominating over one...or several of his pets would have him by the balls. Hard cock, in control, and ready to take a woman to a place only he existed.

But not tonight. His hands balled into fists. He hadn't been able to stop thinking about Evelyn...and how Dario had touched her, had an opportunity to show her more than a sore backside and pinched nipples. But that was all he'd given her.

He raked his fingers through his hair. What the fuck was happening to him? Twenty-four hours ago, he signed a multi-million-dollar deal. Nash was knee deep in shit negotiations. Alex needed a clear head. That's what High Protocol did for him. An outlet for his untapped energy, a place to unwind, focus on a beautiful woman — fuck her hard — and keep his edge.

Evelyn shouldn't be living in his head rent free. Yet he couldn't get her out of his thoughts. He'd considered his options. He could terminate her contract. She was probationary. He could cut her loose from Dario, let her discover for herself what she needed. Uneasiness tightened his gut. She'd end up hurt, unable to recognize the difference between BDSM and abuse.

A weight settled in his gut. None of these would solve his problem. Fuck. He wanted her, and if he didn't put an end to this infatuation, she would only become more of a temptation. He recognized when he was in too deep and depriving himself of something he wanted would only drive him deeper into his obsession.

Evelyn had a lesson with Dario. He spun away from the mirror. Not tonight. Tonight, she was his.

He left his office and approached Ronan. "Have you seen the Professor?"

"Yeah, he went to his room with Tinker."

"Thanks. I'm not going to bother him, but when you see him, tell him to find me."

Tinker. Alex sighed. Not just a regular in the dungeon, she was like a worn, comfortable pair of jeans. Just not his style. Obedient, trained, too trained for Alex. There was no challenge. Perhaps because she'd been in the scene for so long, her mind and body intrinsically responded to a Dom...any Dom. But he recognized Tinker saw him as her protector. In his dungeon, she was safe.

However, Alex needed to work a bit for his rewards. Tinker was too easy. In every way. Hopefully, she'd put Dario into an agreeable mood, because Alex was about to break one of High Protocol's house rules. But what the fuck. It was his dungeon. His rules.

He didn't have to wait long. Fifteen minutes later, Dario popped into his office.

"What's up?"

"Sit down. I want to talk to you."

But like Alex, Dario wasn't comfortable sitting when he could be eye level. He crossed his arms and leaned against the door jamb. "I'm good. Thanks, though."

Alex slipped his hands into his pockets. He'd always gotten along with the Professor, respected his competency as a Dom, but he wouldn't say their association reached the level of friendship. "Evelyn."

A muscle ticked in Dario's jaw. "I'm not surprised."

"Then you won't be surprised when I tell you circumstances have changed."

"Not for me." He cocked a brow. "We have an agreement. Once you assign me a sub, she's mine."

"Not this time."

"Did she complain? Did she cancel her contract?"

"No." She didn't even know of Alex's interest. He'd made it clear he didn't play with inexperienced subs.

"You and I both know she didn't use her safeword." His gaze narrowed. "Until she does, her contract stands." He straightened. "Until I say her training is done."

Alex took a step closer. "We've known each other a long time. We both know how the other operates. I know your rules, and you know mine. But in this case, I'm not asking." That he'd given Dario the courtesy of his intention should have revealed this situation was unique. Not even Alex could explain.

Dario sighed, and the tension seemed to leave his posture. His shoulders relaxed, and his arms dropped to his side. "Just so we're clear, I don't give up my subs. At least, I wouldn't to anyone else." His jaw clenched. "But she's didn't sign a contract with me."

No, her contract was with Alex, and Alex had determined the Professor would be the right Dom for her. A rare occurrence that he'd been wrong. In truth, he'd known yesterday he was making a mistake. Entanglements of the emotional kind made his mouth dry and sent an uncomfortable feeling over him.

"What if she isn't interested?" Dario asked. "Would you let our sub decide who she wants?"

Alex thought about the risk. "Evelyn will always have a choice."

"And if she wants us both?" A hint of a smile curled Dario's lips.

"I don't share." Alex checked his watch. "But tonight, I'll join you in your room." He opened the glass door leading to the outer office.

"Just tonight."

***

Evelyn couldn't focus, couldn't think of anything but the club. The Professor had touched her, touched her in ways that weren't terribly painful…not painful enough. Too many times her body bordered on pleasure. She had become too wrapped up in the moment and hadn't known how to stop the sexual stimulation from taking over.

Actually, she did know how to make it stop, but she hadn't been able to bring herself to say the word Patience, because she hadn't wanted the night to end.

Enduring soft kisses across her stinging buttocks, she'd hoped for more of the sting of the paddle. He'd left her tender and aching. But his invitation offered her more tonight. Power he'd command, and pleasure she'd endure, because that's what he'd need from her.

Last night rolled through her mind. At first, the Professor had overwhelmed her. He was tall, thick, and could have passed for one of the men she'd discovered on the internet. Part of her was grateful. He wasn't her type. Edgy, menacing. He probably rode a motorcycle and made women cry during sex. He was too intense. Too outwardly virile.

For the first time in so long, she felt cracks in her emotions. One night with a stranger had pushed her further than any of the counselors she'd initially seen after Daniel had died. The Professor was better than any anti-depressant pill she'd swallowed.

Evelyn glanced at the clock again. A flash of anxiety heated her belly. Rummaging through her closet, she found a simple black dress. The type every woman had in their closet. Simple two-inch shoulder straps, form fitting, and the hem brushed her legs mid-thigh. A zipper stretched down the back along her spine. Not that she wanted to seduce the Professor. She wanted to make his undressing her easier.

Standing in front of the mirror, she tried to see herself as he must see her. What did he think of a woman who wanted to be punished? Would he see the former paralegal turned recluse or the damaged woman who wanted hurt?

She rolled her eyes at her own assessment. No more damaged than a man must be for wanting to be the one wielding the whip.

This time she approached the club doors with more confidence. Then she smiled. Were subs supposed to feel confident? She slipped inside and smiled at the bouncer. Obviously, he recognized her because he opened the polished black door. "The Boss's instructions are for you to wait at the bar."

"The Boss? I'm supposed to meet with the Professor."

"Mr. Ferraro."

"Oh." Had she done something wrong?

Why would she need to meet with Alex again unless she'd somehow broken the rules of the dungeon?

"Here, Mr. Ferraro is the Boss."

Right. Alex owned the dungeon. Like a child facing disappointment, she entered the nightclub portion of High Protocol. Music pumped through the sound system. This room was also sleek and stylish. It was her understanding that only the Dominants paid membership dues to the club. She hadn't considered the men she encountered would be both powerful and wealthy. An intoxicating combination...for the Dominants.

She didn't care about money. She wasn't looking for a sugar daddy.

"Evelyn."

She turned and her breath caught. She instinctively braced her hand against Alex's chest. "You startled me."

He met her stare as he covered her hand with his and flattened it against his sternum. "My apologies."

His gaze blazed a path lower, first focusing on her mouth, then trailing the rest of the way down her body.

She could do the same to him, but she would have to trail her gaze up those leather clad thighs. She'd have to avoid staring at the bulge of his crotch and the silver glint of the snap on his pants. A tight T-shirt stretched over his toned torso. He wasn't big and muscular like the Professor. Strength simmered in his dark eyes and in the curve of his lips. She'd see all of that if she looked. But no, she wouldn't be as obvious at cataloguing his assets as he was when his gaze raked over her breasts. She wouldn't gawk at the soft wave of his hair or the close cut on the sides.

Then her gaze met his again, and he smiled. Maybe she'd gawked a little. "I'll be late for my session with the Professor."

"Our plans have changed for tonight." He escorted her to the bar. "Would you like a drink?"

She'd remembered the terms of her contract. While probationary and in training, she wasn't allowed to dull her reactions or lose her inhibitions with alcohol or drugs. "Water, I suppose."

She glanced over her shoulder. Where was the Professor? Alex was too attractive, too tempting. His quiet strength unnerved her more than the Professor's imposing presence.

"Good evening, Boss." The bartender set a glass of sparking clear liquid on the counter.

Alex held up two fingers, and the bartender dispersed a matching drink from the fountain.

"Just sparkling water," he said as he handed her the drink. "Are you ready?"

Nervous tension coiled within her. She felt the weight of everyone's stare. Why had Alex brought her into the club? He'd clearly stated she couldn't be here, not until she was ready…until she was trained.

"I'm confused." Was she being trained now? Was she even supposed to speak, and where was the Professor? "Is my training for tonight canceled?"

His hand rested on her lower back. Warmth simmered in her belly as he stood possessively closer. "You have to trust me."

She chewed her bottom lip as they weaved around a couple of tables. "I thought tonight I was supposed to *trust* the Professor."

Trust apparently had many meanings in a dungeon.

His hand curved around to her hip. "Tonight is part of your training."

She furrowed her brows. "Are you taking me to the Professor?"

He chuckled. "You are full of questions."

"As you said, I'm inexperienced." So why was he branding her with his touch? These people were going to think she was his pet. She'd read enough to know some experienced Doms had a kennel full of pets. "Do you want me to keep quiet?"

"Not at all." He led her to a black shiny door at the rear of the club. He punched a code into the door lock, the chambers turned, and the handle released. He held the door for her.

Evelyn stepped into a quiet corridor. "Oh good."

For a moment, she worried he planned to take over her training. How could she hang on to her grief if she couldn't control her thoughts? The intensity in Alex's eyes made her question her reasons for seeking out the club. This wasn't supposed to be about a sexual awakening, not for her.

They paused in front of the door she recognized from the day before.

"Just as yesterday introduced you to the paddle," he said, "tonight is also part of your training."

She nodded. His voice was rich, smooth, and brought erotic images to mind. She imagined he could get a woman to do whatever he asked, whatever he demanded.

The door opened. She scanned the area, her gaze drawn to the steel contraption in the center of the room. A petite woman knelt beneath it. Leather bands strapped to her wrists tethered her hands behind her back. Another strap connected her wrists to her ankles, and her ankles were attached to the steel frame. She wore a black leather mini skirt, the hem barely covering her bottom.

The Professor approached Evelyn. He cupped her cheek. "You look beautiful. How do you feel?"

She shifted her gaze from the Professor to Alex. She felt unsure, confused, nervous, and because of the man still claiming her with his hand to her back, she felt warm. "Is this a group lesson?"

Because she'd tried group therapy and she hadn't handled it well. She had her own issues. She hadn't needed to help anyone else sort out theirs.

"No." Alex's whisper was next to her ear. "This is an observation lesson."

Observation? "You want me to watch?" Because she had watched enough on the internet. Her online education could earn her a degree.

"I want you to watch." Alex took a drink of his seltzer water.

"Are you okay with this?" she asked the Professor. Because yesterday she'd been left with completely different expectations.

The Professor stiffened, and his gaze narrowed on Alex. "He's the Boss."

He turned away and approached the woman on the floor.

Alex took her hand and led her to a large deep-cushioned leather chair in the corner. He set his glass, along with hers, on the table. He sat down and slid back against the high seat. His gaze never wavered from hers. She felt hypnotized, as if she were either poised to fall from a steep cliff or to leap and fly on the wind. Either choice left her vulnerable. Vulnerable to feeling more than the physical pain. She wanted to hurt, to be afraid, not aroused and warm.

"Should I sit on the floor?" Like the

woman with her head tilted back. The Professor had turned her toward them. Teardrop shaped weights dangled from the clamps on her nipples. Evelyn sucked in a breath. Red lips surrounded a black ball strapped into her mouth.

"I want you to sit on my lap."

"On your lap?" While he'd spoken with a decisive controlled request, her response came out as a squeak.

But she would come to learn. She gingerly lowered onto his legs, but Alex gripped her hips and tugged her firmly onto his lap. She sank into the low chair, suddenly realizing just how intimate her encounter with Mr. Ferraro was going to become.

"Relax," he spoke so only she could hear.

His thighs were hard beneath her, the leather of his pants titillating the bare flesh of her legs. The scent of his cologne lingered on the heavy air. Her chest tightened, and her breath came in shallow burst. She tamped down her instinct to fight or flight. She would endure this because when she watched the woman on the floor, cream slicking her thighs as the Professor flicked the stinging tails of a flogger against the porcelain white flesh, Evelyn wanted to be her.

"She's called Tinker," Alex said in hushed tones.

"Because she's petite and blond?"

"Partially."

She leaned against his chest so she could

hear him better. She wanted to know everything about Tinker.

Alex draped his arm across her lap. "They call her Tinker because she's magical. Watch her." His lips feathered against her ear. "Watch her breath catch, her body respond."

The woman on the floor trembled as her arousal permeated the room. "He doesn't have to fuck her to make her come."

Evelyn gasped. Alex's fingers touched the exposed skin of her thigh. She'd worn the dress for the Professor to remove, but Alex brushed his fingertips just under the hem, tracing a soft pattern into her flesh. Her pulse fluttered wildly. She squeezed her thighs together, betrayed by the sensation his hands had on her.

"She is his weakness," he whispered in her ear. "He is her strength."

The professor freed Tinker's arms. He helped her to stand. He gently kissed her fingers, rubbed circulation into her arms, then lifted her limbs over her head and latched the D-rings to the upper, center steel beam of the contraption. Her legs were spread, her arms still immobile, but her body was exposed.

"See the flush on her breasts." Alex shifted.

Evelyn would have closed her eyes and reveled in the feel of his erection pressing into her ass, but in closing her eyes, she'd miss the next snap of the flogger on the back of Tinker's thighs.

"She can't focus. The flogger isn't wielded

to cause her harm. He's stripping away her inhibitions. She's relinquishing control, but in doing so, she finds her own power."

The professor dropped the flogger, released the ball gag from her mouth, and crashed his lips onto hers. He cupped her sex with his palm. Tinker shattered, her body convulsing. She rode the Professor's hand as waves of release rippled through her.

Evelyn's lips parted. Shivers chased over her flesh, but fiery heat rushed through her. Her nipples tightened, and dampness soaked her panties.

Alex grazed her shoulder with his lips. His arm snaked around her waist and crushed her closer. She leaned into him, letting her head tilt as he gently nipped at her neck. Unable to resist the need welling up inside of her, she slightly spread her legs.

He slid a hand onto her inner thigh, pushing her dress into her lap. "You want to be her?"

"Yes," she breathed.

"Is she afraid?" Alex tightened his grip on her leg, his fingers inching a fraction higher.

"No." She swallowed hard.

"But her skin glows." A beautiful crimson blush colored Tinker's shoulders, thighs, and her buttocks.

"She's free." Her voice was barely audible.

"Pain is tearing through her nipples."

Tears filled Evelyn's eyes. "Alex." His name was a plea on her lips. Pressure built within her. Pulses rippled through her sex.

"Look at her." His grip on her tightened.

Evelyn couldn't turn away. Everything she'd seen online had only given her a glimpse into their world. Insecurity seeped into her. Last night, the Professor had given her what she wanted, but Alex wanted more. He wanted her secrets so he could give her what she needed.

The Professor freed Tinker's leg shackles and unhooked her arms. He lifted her. Tinker, with her arms still bound together, curled into his chest.

"Do you think you know who she is? What her secrets are?" His voice lowered even more. "What's next? Will her carry her to bed, climb between her thighs, make tender love to her until he reaches his own release? Or will the Dom in him need to back her up against the wall and fuck her hard and fast?"

Her own breath came hard and fast. Tears trickled onto her cheeks. Cleansing tears, not just for Daniel, but for the woman she'd been. Since Daniel died, she'd lived in hell, her own personal prison. She could have this. More than the pain. But that would mean intimacy. Fear slithered along her spine.

"He's not going to fuck her at all. Tinker is a virgin. The Professor is going to care for her, hold her, and cherish her." Alex cupped Evelyn's cheek, turned her face, and brushed a soft kiss to her lips. "I'll set you free."

"Yes," She was ready to be someone else, anyone else.

Chapter Six

Alex paced across the floor. He needed to tread carefully with Evelyn. Not that he doubted his abilities as a Dom, but he wasn't made of steel. She wasn't one of his pets. She didn't understand the rules. With her, he couldn't play the game.

But he wanted her. Period. And he always got what he wanted.

Nash had connections. In all his dealings, Alex didn't enter into negotiations unless he had all the facts. If he wanted Evelyn's secrets, he'd have to know about her.

"Dig deep," he told Nash over the phone.

Nash was quiet on the other end.

"Is there a problem?"

"Yes, you're the Boss, but I'm not sure I want to go down this rabbit hole with you. Not again."

Alex clenched his jaw. There was no need to discuss ancient history.

"Go to the dungeon," Nash said. "Play with one of your pets."

He could play until every muscle in his body was spent...including his dick. But a pet wouldn't quench his desire for Evelyn. "Evelyn Larsen." He gave Nash the rest of her information from the questionnaire.

Nash sighed. "I love you, brother."

They disconnected. He didn't need to say anything else.

After Siara—just thinking her name was a punch to the gut—Alex had fallen into a dark place. Betrayal cut like a knife. Any version of love he might have thought he felt for her had burned along with the trust. After the breakup, he'd opened High Protocol and played exclusively with his pets.

Now, Nash was the only person he trusted. And he trusted him implicitly.

Even though gathering the information would take a couple of days, Alex wasn't waiting. He wasn't asking Nash for information to find a way out of his developing feelings for Evelyn. He wanted more.

Joel entered Alex's office. "She's here."

Alex nodded. "Take her to my rooms."

He tugged on his tie, loosening the knot. A smile curled his lips as he went through his personal entrance to the private rooms of the dungeon.

His Italian leather oxfords echoed of the marble tiled floor as he strode to the end of the hall. He paused in front of the double doors. His reflection shown in the polished black lacquer finish. He sucked in a calming breath, although inside, adrenaline rushed through him. He opened the door.

Evelyn turned in his direction. God, she

was beautiful. With every tilt of her head, the light caught the subtle variations in her sexy tangle of hair. Long lashes lowered as she glanced away from him.

He crossed to her, hooked a finger under her chin, and lifted her face. "Whenever we see each other, I'll expect a kiss hello."

"A kiss?" she questioned.

He smiled. "To show me you're happy to see me." He brought his face closer to hers. Her lips quivered, and her subtle perfume tickled his senses. "Are you?"

As her answer, she gently brushed her lips against his. The whisper of a kiss sent a fierce craving surging through him. He wanted to crush his mouth to hers, strip her of her barriers, and bury his cock in her heat. Instead, he slipped his hand into hers and led her to the mirrored bar. A long counter stretched along the wall. While he didn't drink, he still stocked the finest liquor in his private rooms. He opened the small fridge and grabbed two small bottles of water.

"I want to renegotiate your contract." He handed her one of the bottles.

"I see."

He unscrewed the cap and took a sip. "I think you do." He leaned back against the counter. "I'm not like the Professor. I'm not interested in training you for someone else."

She swallowed and licked her lips.

"You'll belong to me."

Her brow arched. "Belong to you?"

Her pulse fluttered in her neck. Her fingers fidgeted with the cap on the water bottle. But her focus was on him. Her gaze softened, and her lips slightly parted.

"Our relationship won't be confined to the dungeon. We'll go out, have dinner, and socialize."

"That sounds more like dating."

"No, we won't be dating." He took a step closer to her. "Dating implies you could date other men. You'll be exclusively mine, inside and outside the club."

"I only came to the club to—"

"I know why you came to the club." He leaned in and kissed her jaw. His lips trailed to her ear and then slipped along her neck. "I promise, I know what you need."

She sucked in a breath as she braced her hands on his hips, her fingers gripping to him. "If I say yes…"

"I'm listening."

"If I say yes to being your submissive, I'll kiss you." Her voice trembled. "Not just for hello. I'll kiss you to show you I've surrendered my control to you." She released a shuddering exhale. "And I'll trust you," she quietly said. "But I don't want to have sex."

He smiled and cupped her cheek. He brushed his lips against hers. "You will."

Her lips parted, and he slid in for a dark

erotic taste. His tongue slipped into her mouth, touching hers and demanding passion in return.

Alex broke the kiss. "I assume you agree."

"Yes."

"We'll need a name for you."

"What's wrong with Evelyn?"

"You have a beautiful name. Do your friends call you Evie?"

She nodded. "And my family. But I don't want you to call me that, at least not here in the club. I don't see why I need another name."

"The names remind us of our roles while in a scene."

"But I'll be yours. I won't forget my role."

The words hit him hard. His gut tumbled. He took her hand and led her to the adjoining room.

"I met the Professor and understand he's a trainer. What are you called?"

He chuckled. "I assumed you guessed. I'm the Boss."

"Oh." She smiled. "I assumed...I just assumed they were calling you Boss since you owned the dungeon." She paused just inside the room, then slowly made her way around the perimeter. An assortment of paraphernalia and props for pain and punishment lined one wall. But the majority of his equipment focused on bondage. Leather collars and cuffs, restraints, and tools for sensory deprivation.

Alex came up behind her. He rested his

hands on her shoulders. "When you come to my playroom, I want you in a skirt or dress, no panties." He tugged on the hem of her top. She lifted her arms, and he slipped it over her head. "I'll undress you." He kissed her bare shoulder and tugged her bra strap onto her arm. He lowered the other strap. "I like to open my gifts."

"You see me as your gift?"

He grazed his thumb across the tip of her breast through the lace of her bra. Her nipple hardened. "Absolutely."

"Will I need to call you Boss?"

He turned her toward him and stared into her eyes. "Will you forget my role?"

Her eyes widened with innocence. "Never, Alex. I won't forget my role or yours. I know what I'm saying yes to."

"And that is?"

"I'm saying yes to you."

He unhooked her bra. "And I can kiss you whenever…and wherever I want?"

The bra fell forward catching in the crook of her elbows. "Yes."

Alex bent and closed his mouth over the tightened nipple, sucking her smooth, hot flesh into his mouth. He dropped to his knees and unsnapped her jeans. He drank in the scent of her flesh as he pressed a kiss to her taut belly. Then he peeled the denim down her legs.

Abstaining from sex would kill him. He wanted more than her submission. Longing, raw and primal roared within him. He was on dangerous ground, risking more than his sanity. He risked his heart. She wasn't a Tinker. A sexual woman burned beneath the surface. He wouldn't be content with pieces. He needed her as desperate as he felt. But not today. The choice was hers...and always would be. But that didn't mean he couldn't be convincing. He had a playroom full of weapons to tear down her armor.

"Everything off. Everything." He looked up into her face as he fingered the edge of her panties. As he tugged them down her legs, he relished the feel of her smooth skin. He lifted one foot and then the other for her to step out of her shoes.

Alex stood and crossed to his leather and tools. With an experienced sub, he wouldn't need to worry about the restraints being too tight or the confinement too intense. Evelyn wanted rough and painful. He was going to give her seductive, intense, and pleasurable. She might not want sex, but he was going to make her come.

And he was going to show her he understood her need to hurt. He would hurt her...because they both needed the release.

He grasped a pair of leather manacles. He pressed his lips to her pulse point before wrapping the leather securely around her wrist. "Remember, your safeword stops everything."

An audible swallow, then she nodded.

"Submission doesn't make you weak." He led her to a steel wall. D-rings, spaced twelve inches apart, ran parallel to the ceiling. More hooks, approximately ten feet apart ran vertically up the wall. To the left, a selection of chains dangled from large C-hooks, and to the right, an assortment of whips hung from their handles.

Evelyn's eyes widened as she crossed in front of the whips and then stared at the cold steel.

"This is what you want?" he asked.

She bowed her head. Her chest rose and fell with her rapid, shallow breathing. "Yes."

"The first strike will take your breath." He whispered close to her ear, grazing his lips along her neck. "The second will sting." He took her wrist and pulled a section of chain through the metal ring on the manacle. "Turn around."

She faced the wall, trembling.

"Are you afraid?"

Evelyn licked her lips. "Yes." She glanced into his eyes. "But not of you. And not of the pain. I want you to hurt me." Her gaze pleaded with him to understand. "But I'm afraid you won't."

"I'll hurt you so long as the pain brings you pleasure. I won't abuse you." Did she understand there was a difference? He leaned in and touched the seam of her lips with his tongue. She sucked in a sharp little inhale.

Alex stretched the chains to the D-hooks

above her. She rested her forehead against the cool steel, her arms creating a wide V over her head. He repeated the process to her legs, spreading them just wider than shoulder width apart and then chaining her to the wall.

He trailed his fingers over the round curve of her smooth, heart-shaped ass. His fingers trailed lower, sliding between her thighs. "I want to touch you here." His finger slid between her folds.

She rolled her forehead, side to side, against the steel.

He paused. "Is that a no?" He waited for her to answer.

"Whip me first," she whispered.

Alex had several whips, but the thirty-six-inch bullwhip with the hard, leather wrapped handle and the woven tail gave him the most control. One stinging stripe at a time. He cracked the whip against the wall. She jumped, a little yelp slipping from her at the startling sound. He curled his fingers around the warm leather and struck the wall again in the same spot. He wanted her to see, from the arc of the woven tail, he mastered control of the whip.

He flipped his arm to the side. The tail whistled through the quiet room and painted a line across the flat of her scapula. Evelyn moaned, and her shoulders bunched. Another stripe landed one inch below the first.

Her hands tightened into fists.

The next three snaps of the whip came in quick succession.

Evelyn cried out, her body pressing against the cold steel.

Sweat slipped along his spine, and his cock hardened. She was breathtakingly beautiful. Powerful in her acceptance of the pain. He repeated the strikes to mark her left side. The bright red flesh puckered with thin precision welts, creating a perfectly symmetrical pattern of ridges.

Evelyn gasped. She sank her teeth into her lower lip.

Alex dropped the whip, crossed the space, and crashed his lips onto hers. He plunged his tongue into her mouth, stealing her breath and relishing in her submission. His fist tangled in her hair as he ate at her mouth, sliding his tongue against hers. He growled, gently biting her lower lip, the same way she'd bitten down during the thrashes.

"Can I touch you now?" He closed his palm over her pussy. "So wet," he said sliding his finger into her hot, moist center.

Evelyn moaned, her head lolling to the side. She couldn't focus, her eyes rolling and her lids sliding closed.

"Alex," she whispered, shuddering quivers liquefying her legs. She wobbled, clinging to the chains.

He released the buckle on one wrist

manacle, then the other. Her limbs dropped to her side. She braced against the wall as he dropped to his knee and freed each of her legs. Without hesitation, he scooped her into his arms and carried her to the bed. With one hand, he jerked the covers down.

"Sit here." He placed her near the top of the bed. Lifting her hand, he forced her fingers to curl around the iron frame at the corner of the bondage bed. Alex crossed to the bar and ran a thin cloth under cold water. Then he filled a glass with ice, grabbed a dry soft towel, and his bottle of aloe gel.

"I'll take care of you," he said as he placed the supplies on the end table. Sitting next to her on the bed, he carefully positioned her more fully on the bed, her back to him. Taking a piece of ice between his fingers, he slowly traced the angry hot welts.

She flinched from the cold but sighed as the ice melted against her skin. Water droplets trickled along her back, following the contours of her ribs and spine. Alex tasted a drip of water from her flesh before softly kissing her marks.

She shivered against his lips.

"Evelyn, look at me."

She slowly turned her face, her gaze struggling to lock on his face.

Alex traced her lips with the ice. "Suck."

She curled her delicate fingers around his wrist and closed her hot mouth over his icy fingers. Her eyes slid closed as the ice melted in her mouth. Emotions welled in his gut. He took her mouth, savoring the taste of her cooled tongue.

Yet, her body continued to tremble.

He quickly but gently applied the aloe gel to her abrasions. His strikes had been perfect. By morning she might have slight bruising from the restraints, but the whip hadn't broken the skin. She'd wear the stripes for a few days, but the welts wouldn't linger. Draping the cold cloth over her back, he further cooled her skin.

"Lie down." He slid in next to her, covering them both with the heated, weighted blanket. He pulled her into his chest, holding her and resting his lips against her temple. "You were beautiful," he whispered, hoping she recognized the exchange they'd just shared. He hadn't made her come, but she hadn't needed that kind of release. She needed to know his brand of hurt, pleasure pain, could feel just as good.

She pressed closer, her arms tucked in front of her and curled into his chest. Careful of her back, he held her tightly.

A shuddering, deep exhale softened her posture. Her head tilted as she stared into his eyes. "Thank you."

"My pleasure, Evie."

She smiled.

Chapter Seven

Evelyn stood at the kitchen window. The late afternoon sun dipped low on the horizon. Evening was approaching and so was her anticipation. One night with the Professor hadn't prepared her for a lesson with Alex. In only a few days, he'd shattered her world into a million little pieces. Nothing seemed the same. When she was with him, she didn't feel lost, or overwhelmed with grief. But then she'd come home, and like a heavy cape, the darkness cloaked her again. Part of her wondered if this was some developing sick form of co-dependency.

In her training, she'd learned not to question him. She'd been with him, in his lair, feeling the sting of his kiss whether from a whip or braided flogger…or from his deliciously wicked mouth. She hadn't wanted to have sex, didn't want to lose herself completely. But then she'd drowned in the liquid euphoria of being under his control.

The doorbell pulled her from her musings. Just because she'd gone to the dungeon, didn't mean her home life had changed much. Maybe it had. She couldn't focus on her work because she couldn't get Alex off her mind.

She opened the door. "Hi."

Misty came through the door. "Oh good,

you are home."

"Where would I go?" Evelyn said.

"I don't know, but I've stopped by a few nights, and you haven't been home. You don't answer the phone either. You owe me. Jane called me to come do a welfare check. Your mom is about to call the police to come check on you." She strode into the house, dropped her purse on the couch, and headed toward the kitchen. "Do you have anything to eat? I'm starving."

Evelyn followed her. "Probably not."

Misty had her head in the fridge. She glanced over the top of the door. "No wonder you're thin. There is nothing to eat in here."

Evelyn smiled. Misty was always bubbly, the happy sort that smiled and laughed.

"I'm sorry you had to come over."

"You could have saved me if you'd answer your phone and talk your family once in a while." She closed the fridge.

"I have talked to my mom, but all she wants to talk about are ways to fix me. And Jane... Don't get me started on my sister. I'm not trying to be difficult. But I don't want to spend all day talking about her love life, marriage, and happily ever afters. Not to say I'm not happy for her. I am. I've even agreed to be in the wedding, but it's not until next year."

Misty crossed her arms over her chest, covering the saying *I Licked It, So It's Mine*, written across the front. She flipped her brown shoulder length locks out of her eyes. "Like me, they care about you. But you're stubborn." She ticked off Evelyn's character traits—or flaws—on her finger. "I can go on. You're a picky eater. You hate to go to the movies. You listen to disco music. You dress like shit. You'd think you're sixty not twenty-six."

"I get it. I'm not that pathetic."

"I'd say you can add reclusive and boring, but you haven't been home, at night, all week, so something is up."

Evelyn rolled her eyes. "I have been getting out more." She took two mugs from the cupboard. "Coffee?"

"Yes, so tell me. I can be pacified with a few tidbits."

Evelyn tried to think fast. She couldn't very well share what she'd really been doing. How would Misty react to hearing, *I went online and developed an obsession with BDSM. Now, I'm a sub in training, and apparently, I've given myself to a Master and he's determined to make me his. I spend every night in his dungeon as he ties me up and makes me come whether I want to or not. And strangely, I want to, and I am scared to admit I want more.*

"I have been going out. I found a new place. I've been hanging out there…and I've met someone."

"Really? Oh Evie, tell me everything." She dropped onto a kitchen chair, kicked off her shoes, and rested her elbows on the table.

"There is nothing to tell. Especially to my mom and sister." She brought two mugs of coffee to the table. "Please. I don't want expectations, and I don't want you worrying about me anymore."

"Then tell me what he's like. What's his name?"

"Alex." Evelyn thought of Alex, as if she could get him off her mind. "He's serious…and private." Strong, controlling, demanding, but tender. And he was breathtakingly handsome. His seductive voice could make her body tremble and her heart race.

"I don't believe it." Misty covered her mouth with her hand.

"What?"

"You have the look, the glazed eyes, the faraway look that says you're with him, even when you're not. How long have you known him? Where did you meet him?"

"Not long and—" Think. She couldn't tell Misty where she'd met him or really much about him. "I met him online."

"You went from recluse to online dating? Evie, it's dangerous. I mean, I'm glad you're moving on, but don't be stupid."

"I'm careful." What more could she say. The control wasn't hers to exert. She was his. When he wanted her naked, bound in his room, her arms strapped to the St. Andrews Cross as he kissed her flesh with the tails of the flogger, she

73

wouldn't refuse him. She wouldn't want to.

"Then spend more time with him but stay in public places."

She preferred the safety and security of his private playroom. "It's not serious."

"Use protection. Online dating is nothing but manwhores."

"I'm not sleeping with him. And I said I met him online but not online dating. It's complicated. Just know that I've found something that I've needed for a while."

"Okay. I won't bitch. I'm glad you're dating."

"We're not dating." They'd clearly determined that already.

"Whatever. Just remember you set the boundaries. You make the rules."

No, Misty was completely off the mark with that one, too. Evelyn may have set the boundaries, defining the hard and soft limits. Her tummy tumbled. Yes, she'd relinquished all control to Alex.

Before she could answer anymore of Misty's questions, the doorbell rang. She wasn't expecting anyone. Misty crossed the room and opened the door.

Evelyn froze. Her gaze darted between the manager from the club and her best friend.

"Hi," she stammered and scrambled around Misty.

"This must be Alex." Misty opened the

door wider. "Are you going to introduce us?"

"No." He chuckled. "I'm not Alex."

Misty's eyes widened. "Oh."

Evelyn wasn't even sure of the man's name, but she wouldn't forget the face or the body. Her brain went dead, and she forgot her own name. She gazed past him to the driveway. "Why are you here?"

"Come in. I'm Misty." Her eyebrow arched. "You aren't Alex?"

The man entered the room. "Ronan." His gaze raked up Misty's body, and a smile spread across his face.

Evelyn shifted from one foot to the other, tilting her head coyly to the side. Oh no, this was not happening. Misty flirted with the manager to her BDSM club. This was a disaster.

"Did Alex send you?" Evelyn found her voice and inserted herself between Misty and Ronan.

"Yes, this is from the Boss." He held out a large black and red gift bag. "Wear this and be ready at six."

Evelyn peered into the bag. She lifted the slip of a dress from the bag.

"Oh, that is hot." Misty fingered the sheer fabric. "Alex has excellent tastes, although I'm not sure he has you figured out," she said to Evelyn.

"This from the woman who uses T-shirts as billboards."

Misty shrugged and winked at Ronan.

"He said you would remember the rules," Ronan said to Evelyn.

"Rules?" Misty snapped her gaze to Evelyn.

Misty had heard enough. She was bound to start asking more questions, and Evelyn had run out of vague replies. She snatched the dress back from Misty and dropped it back in the bag. "Um, you can let Alex know I'll be there at nine, and he can have this back."

"He insisted on six."

"Give him my apologies, but I have a dinner engagement. We are dining at Tuscany this evening."

"We are?" Misty asked.

Evelyn narrowed her gaze. "Yes, we are."

"He won't be pleased."

A shiver slipped over her skin. Punishment was what she wanted.

Once the door closed and Ronan was gone, Evelyn released a deep exhale.

"So what was all that about?" Misty flopped onto the couch. "Is Alex some kind of control freak?"

"Yes, I'd say he has control issues. But he knows what he wants."

"Like I said, you need to be careful. You need to find someone successful who can sweep you off your feet and take you to some exotic place."

Alex did just that. Not in the way Misty

imagined. Evelyn would be swept off her feet into a suspension rack, the exotic location was a private room…taking her to subspace.

"If we are going to Tuscany, get changed. I'm starving."

Evelyn hurried to the rear of the house to the master bedroom. Only a week ago, she'd been wallowing in her depression. Now, adrenaline coursed through her. Defying Alex would come with a cost. Risk versus reward. She'd risked his ire, knowing she'd be rewarded in his private rooms.

Evelyn stripped off her sweatshirt and opened her closet door. She wouldn't have time to come home, shower, and change. She skimmed through her closet, selecting a summer dress she could wear without a bra. The halter tied behind her neck, and the skirt shimmied along her body, draping nearly to her feet. She glanced down to her arms and wrists. Red marks crisscrossed her wrists. She spun in the mirror. She had a few bruises on her back, but the marks of the whip had faded to light, barely noticeable stripes. Although no one would see, she did have dark purple bruises on her hips, but not from Alex, rather from the hard frame of the cross.

"What the fuck?" Misty stood at the threshold to her room. Her mouth opened, and her brows pinched. Her mouth formed a distressed line. "What the fuck happened to you?"

Evelyn squealed and spun around. "Don't scare me!"

Misty stormed across the room and did a quick inspection of her body. She grabbed her wrist. "Don't tell me you did this to yourself. You couldn't have put those bruises on your back. Or here." She touched the back of Evelyn's upper arm.

Evelyn twisted in the mirror. The bruises weren't dark, but she did have slight discoloration from the cuffs Alex had used to pin her arms behind her back.

"Don't you have anything to say?"

No, because if she told Misty the truth, she'd judge her...or she'd judge Alex. Evelyn had sought out the dungeon. "I'm fine."

"You said you weren't sleeping with him."

"I'm not."

"That's abuse."

It wasn't. Alex was firm but gentle. He wasn't beating her up, but rather he was tearing down her walls.

"Does he hurt you?"

"No." Yes, but only in ways that made her crave more. "It's not what you think."

"Evie, I'm scared for you." Tears filled Misty's eyes. "Are you in trouble?"

Evelyn sat on the edge of the bed. She folded her hands in her lap. She'd signed a non-disclosure agreement. She couldn't talk about Alex, the dungeon, or the dark temptations hidden within. Somehow, she had to make Misty understand without breaking her agreement.

"I wish you could just trust me. Everyone was on me to move on, let Daniel go, get out, start dating, fall in love, get married one day, have a family, get a new job, snap out of it, get out of the house—"

"I get it. But I don't think any of us would have thought you'd settle for an abusive relationship."

Her head bowed. "It's not." She released a shaky exhale. "Not what you think." She'd have to tell her something. "I'm in a D/s relationship."

"Shut the fuck up."

Evelyn snapped her head up. "Yes. I found it online while I was doing research for work."

"So you found someone online to smack you around a bit?"

"No, of course not. I found a private club, and no, I can't talk to you about it. I signed a non-disclosure."

"Because the assholes who like to beat up on women know it's illegal. Big biker types with tattoos and piercings."

Evelyn rolled her eyes. "You won't understand, and you don't have to. If you want a vanilla relationship, that's fine."

Misty erupted with a laugh. "Are you seriously using BDSM language on me? A vanilla relationship? And what are you into, rocky road, salted caramel, twisted chocolate? Whatever it is, it must have nuts, because you'd have to be nuts to want some dick to bend you over and spank your ass. That shit is for people with problems. They live in their own fantasy that it's normal. I'm smart enough to know it's not normal. It's sick and twisted. I thought you were smarter, too."

"I'm not going to try to convince you of anything." She met her best friend's gaze. "I was dying inside." Tears filled her eyes. "I don't care if you think it's crazy, abusive, or wrong. I know it's none of those things. When I'm with Alex, I don't think of Daniel or the past. I just want to be with him...all the time. I trust him to know what I need. And he doesn't hurt me."

He did, but he didn't cause her harm. Misty wouldn't understand because she'd never trusted someone else with her power or control.

Evelyn recognized now, she'd been Daniel's sub. They didn't have bondage or punishment, but he had power over her. She needed that, and when she lost him, she lost herself.

Misty shook her head. "What if something goes wrong? You could get hurt."

She hurt before BDSM, trapped in her grief. Alex was setting her free. "Or I can finally be free of the hurt."

Chapter Eight

Alex stared at the returned gift.

"She had a friend there." Ronan slid his hands into his pockets.

"Male or female?"

"Girlfriend. They were heading over to Tuscany for dinner, and she said she'd see you at nine." Ronan raised a brow at Alex, then slipped out the door.

Alex sat alone in his office with his thoughts. In a few days, Evelyn had listened, learned, and responded. But they'd remained in the dungeon. Tonight, Alex had tested her limits. A smile curled his lips. His pet wanted a spanking.

He grabbed his key fob from the top drawer of his desk. He hesitated on taking the gift with him but decided against it. She didn't have to wear the dress. He preferred her naked anyway.

"I won't be back," he said to Joel as he left the building through the door leading to the private parking garage. He climbed behind the wheel of his black sports sedan, sitting low in the bucket seats. He put on his sunglasses, peeled out of his personal parking spot, and squealed out of the garage.

Dusk cast a golden glow over the city.

Dark tinted windows cut through the glare. He'd been to Tuscany many times. Italian food with a nice outdoor seating section and only a few blocks from his downtown offices. His fingers curled around the steering wheel as he shifted into third and turned a corner as if on a racetrack. The car, low to the ground, hugged the road.

He pulled into valet parking and handed over his keys. Entering the restaurant, he smiled at the hostess, strode through the indoor dining area, and crossed to the patio.

As if she sensed his arrival, Evelyn glanced over to where he stood. He couldn't hear the words, but he still understood when she said, "oh, shit," to her friend.

The dark-haired woman looked over her shoulder.

Alex crossed the room. Adrenaline surged through his body. Part of him worried that she wasn't ready, ready for her role. He approached the table, projecting outward calm, but a thousand thoughts hammered inside his head. This was a risk, but one he needed to take if he was going to continue with Evelyn. In truth, he was fucked. Because he'd already lost. She owned him.

Stopping at the table, he slipped off his sunglasses, and his gaze connected with hers. Moments lasted an eternity. His heartbeat raced, but the world seemed to slow. And then she scooted her chair back, stood, and leaned into him.

She rose on her tiptoes and softly kissed his lips. "Hello, Alex."

Inside, he melted. He touched her cheek. He could tell her he was in the neighborhood or going to his office, but they both know he'd be lying, and he wanted trust and honesty with her. "I missed you."

She smiled and then turned to her friend. "This is Misty Kemp."

"A pleasure." He shook her hand.

"You might not think so—"

Evelyn bumped her hip against the table. Water sloshed out of the crystal goblets. Misty grabbed her glass of wine before it could tip.

"We haven't ordered yet. Can you join us?"

"Thank you." He held the chair for Evelyn, then took the seat next to her. "If you haven't tried it, their gnocchi Sorrento is delicious as is the cappelletti in brodo."

Misty took a drink of her wine. "You must come here often."

"My office is on Third."

"Ah, your office." Misty nodded as if she agreed with him. "Do you typically order for your dates or office lunches?" She leaned in and snidely spoke to him. "I mean, that's the sort of thing you are into, right? Among other things." The table jolted. "Ouch!" She snapped her gaze to Evelyn. "Did you just kick me?"

"Sorry, my foot slipped." She glanced to Alex. "I'll try the gnocchi."

"She's adventurous, wouldn't you say? Trying new things. I mean, I barely know her anymore."

"Misty, I did kick you, and I'll kick you again. Shut up."

Alex leaned back in the chair. He slowly smiled.

"Do you think this is funny?" Misty narrowed her gaze. "Have you seen her body?"

"I have."

"Stop." Evelyn slapped her hand to the table. "This is not happening." She blinked, keeping tears from her eyes. Her lips trembled, and she nervously glanced from Alex to Misty, to the doorway.

He reached under the table and rested his hand on her thigh. "I'm not upset. I'm crashing your dinner engagement. You can be angry with me."

She was clearly angry with her friend, probably embarrassed, and because of the newness of their association, unsure of how to explain their relationship.

"Would you punish her if you were?"

"Misty!"

"If you want to know if I would harm her, then I can put your mind at ease. Never."

"Then how do you explain the bruises on her arms and back? Have you seen her wrists?"

Evelyn slid her chair back. "I'm sorry," she said to Alex. She turned to Misty. "How could you? I shared something intimate and personal to me, and you are practically shouting about it in a restaurant. I asked you to trust me."

Misty's expression softened, and her shoulders slumped. "Evie, I...I..."

The server approached. "Ready to order?"

"Evelyn." The tone of his voice demanded her attention. "The gnocchi?"

She nodded and scooted her chair back in.

"Misty, have you decided?" he asked.

She glanced at the menu, then turned and glared. "The fettuccini."

"And I'll have the cappelletti."

The server took the menus.

"And coffee please." Once she'd stepped away, Alex leaned back in his chair and crossed one foot over his knee. "Evelyn trusted you enough to tell you about us. I trust her, so if you have questions, ask."

Misty folded and unfolded the napkin in front of her on the table. "Do you hurt her?"

He inhaled, considered his response, and slowly exhaled. "Yes."

Her brows pinched. "Why? She's hurt enough."

"An athlete pushes through pain. A mountain climber will endure bitter cold, and a rock climber risks life and limb. Why do any of us endure pain and discomfort? Because all of us, the human spirit, wants to push past that threshold, feel the rush, savor the pleasure."

"Evie—"

"No, ask me." If Evelyn wanted to share her experiences with Misty, that was her decision. He knew she wouldn't break the clauses of the contract. But Misty's issues were with him.

"Is that your rule? She can't speak unless you allow her to?"

"I don't need her to defend me."

"Are you trying to seduce her?"

"Absolutely." The coffee and salads arrived at the table.

Once the server left, Evelyn spoke. "You're not seducing me."

But not even she sounded convinced.

He took a sip of his coffee, savoring the hot, strong brew.

"I want to know more," Misty said. "I want to know what you do to her."

Alex shook his head and laughed. "No, that isn't open for discussion."

A blush tinted Evelyn's cheeks.

Misty grimaced. "I guess I don't need to wonder if she enjoys what you do to her." She lowered her voice as if she were talking to herself. "I knew she was full of shit when she said it wasn't sexual."

Alex shifted his gaze back to Evelyn. He would like to know what else she said. Her definition of sexual and his must be different.

Tonight, in the dungeon, he'd make sure she understood. Just because he hadn't fucked her didn't mean her orgasms didn't fall under the definition of a sexual relationship.

The meal arrived. Misty's questions distanced from BDSM and his bedroom sports to his work.

"I'm a venture capitalist."

"You put money into startups?"

"Sometimes. I supposed I'm also a liquidator. If a company is worth more in pieces than a whole, I'll acquire enough stock for a takeover, or I'll buy it outright to sell it off."

Misty twisted fettuccini noodles onto her fork. "You aren't what I expected."

"In what way?"

She shrugged. "When Evie told me she was dating a Dom, I assumed a guy with control issues. Well, maybe you do have control issues. But you appear to be a normal, good-looking guy. Not someone who takes advantage of emotionally damaged women. I told her to get a hot guy, preferably one with enough money that he didn't need hers." She stuffed more noodles into her mouth.

"You told her we were dating?" He smiled at Evelyn.

"No." Her eyes narrowed on Misty. "I specifically told her we were not dating." She stabbed her fork into a gnocchi.

He leaned into her. "Did you tell her we

were exclusive?" He opened his mouth. Without hesitation, she fed him a bite of her dinner. "That I prefer a woman who knows her own mind, who isn't afraid to ask for what she wants?"

"I didn't. I wouldn't have told her anything if you hadn't sent Ronan to collect me with that horrible dress." She glanced down at what she had on. With the jacket over the halter dress, she was covered from breasts to toes.

"Too short?" he asked of the gift.

One eyebrow arched. "Maybe a little."

"Noted."

"Next time, I'll get you something to wear around your neck."

"I love jewelry," Misty said. "I had this awesome rose quartz pendant, but my incredibly wild boyfriend Minty broke the chain, and I haven't been able to find it."

"Minty and Misty?"

Evelyn chuckled. "Her cat. He's awful. He hates everyone except her. I refuse to ever house sit her cat again. His hiss is pure evil, and he attacked my leg. I have the scars to prove it."

Misty swallowed another bite of food. "Hmm. I thought you would have liked that. You said it was painful." She smiled as she shrugged her shoulders. "Sorry, I couldn't resist."

When the server brought the check, Alex handed her his card.

"I've got it." Evelyn reached for her purse.

"It's my pleasure. I've had a lovely dinner,

ladies." He checked his watch.

"I'll see you at nine," Evelyn said. She took the napkin from her lap and laid it on the table.

"Did you drive?"

"Yes, and I have to take Misty home. She had wine with her dinner."

"Half a glass," Misty said, pointing to her wine glass. "It's too dry for me. I'm fine." She straightened her shoulders and cocked her head to the side. "I'm not going to pretend to understand this kinky shit you're into, but I'm going to trust you know what you want. I never liked ice cream, so I guess if you want nuts in yours, it's not my business." She snuck a glance at Alex. "But I'm also going to inspect her and if things get too—" She hunched her shoulders. "— too rough, I'll put an end to it." She locked gazes with Evelyn. "I'll tell your mom." She held out her palm. "I'll drive myself home, and we can hook up later to get your car back."

Evelyn slid her hand into the side pocket of her purse. Then she handed the keys to Misty. "Are you sure?"

Misty lowered her voice. "I don't know what you're doing, but you're not sitting alone at home. Be careful. I know his name, where he works, and I know what he is. If you go missing, he's prime suspect number one. So if you don't want me doing welfare checks on you, answer your phone and let me know you're safe." Her voice softened. "Then I won't worry."

Alex pulled his cell from his pocket. "Misty, what is your number?"

She spouted off the number, and a moment later, her phone pinged. "I sent you my contact information." Her phone pinged again. "And that is my business partner, Nash Corbett. He always knows where I am."

Evelyn's brows furrowed. "I don't have your business partner's number."

"Okay, I guess that means you won't be hiding the body anywhere." She smirked and twirled the keys. She gave Evelyn a quick hug. "I'd tell you to have fun, but I don't think I want to contribute to your delinquency." She waved. "Thanks for dinner," she said to Alex as she walked away.

"Ready?" he asked

She nodded. He put his hand on her lower back and escorted her through the restaurant. Once outside, he handed his ticket to the valet.

She shifted from one foot to the other. "I'm sorry about tonight."

He wasn't. Tonight, he'd learned a lot about where her head was at regarding their association. Yes, she responded to him. But she'd responded to the Professor as well. Was she just another Tinker in the making?

"She's like a sister."

"Evelyn, I'm not upset." A muscle ticked in his jaw. Anticipation simmered hot and dangerous in his gut. "I'm pleased."

She glanced up into his face. "But I skirted the confidentiality clause. I didn't mention the club or anything that we've done. But I told her about you...about us."

The car pulled up to the curb. The attendant exited the driver's side. Alex bent and opened the passenger door for her. As she stood in the opening, he closed the space between them. "Why was I pleased?"

Her delicate pink tongue touched her lower lip. She swallowed. He ached to taste her, to kiss her again, but this time, take her mouth in a way that left no misunderstanding of his plans of seduction.

"Because I kissed you."

"Were you happy to see me?"

"Maybe not right at that moment." Her soft mellifluous laugh seeped into him, sending fissions of desire along his spine. "But I still wanted to kiss you."

"Kiss me now."

Her gaze rested on his lips. She leaned in. Warm breath caressed his lips. Her hands slid along his waist, her touch gentle and hesitant. She started with a whisper of a kiss, barely brushing his lips with hers. Then her lips slightly parted, and she pressed into his lips with hers. He groaned, opened his mouth, and claimed her. His arm snaked around her waist and pulled her flush against him. He conquered her tongue with his, sliding into her mouth, and taking taste after taste. He rolled his hips, letting her feel the heat and hardness of his erection against her.

A car horn bleeped several times. Alex broke the kiss and glanced to the street. Misty drove down the road, arm out the window waving.

"Let's go home," he said.

"Home?"

"My place." He wanted her naked, bound, a blush to her buttocks, and writhing beneath him. At least he'd get three out of the four.

Chapter Nine

His place. The words settled in her belly and churned there. She hadn't been fully honest with Misty or herself. She wasn't simply in a contracted arrangement. Rippling currents of desire were trying to pull her under. Going to the dungeon was like going to the therapist or a trip to the spa. At High Protocol, her role was easily defined...and so was Alex's. She wasn't prepared for home schooling.

She glanced through the darkened passenger window at the downtown skyscrapers. He turned into the private underground parking garage. The car's engine hummed in the hollow space.

He made a couple of turns and then parked. He turned to her. "Ready?"

She wasn't sure, but she nodded.

Alex exited the car then came around to her side and opened her door. She walked next to him into a beautiful lobby. A security guard said hello as Alex led her toward the bank of polished steel elevators. He pushed the up button. The doors dinged, opened. and they stepped inside. He tapped a card to the control panel. A green light lit the icon PH for the fortieth floor. He lived in the penthouse.

The elevator doors opened to his

apartment. Automatic lights illuminated the foyer. He placed his hand on her back, escorting her inside. He dropped his keys on the marble table. "Your jacket?"

She shifted her shoulders and removed her jacket. He hung it on the empty brushed steel coat tree next to the door. His fingers grazed her shoulder and trailed along her arm. He reached her hand, lifted her wrist, and kissed the red marks left by his restraints. His tongue tasted her pulse point, sending flares of heat into her sex.

Fear sizzled over her flesh. This was dangerous, threatening her heart. Inside the club, she understood the rules. With their contract, she agreed to be in his world. But finding her at the restaurant, sharing his contact information, and chatting it up with her best friend, kissing him—and wanting more—was spinning her wildly out of control. The little bit of power she wanted to hold onto slipped away. In everything he said and did, he made it clear he wanted more than her initiation into submission. Was she ready to be in his life?

He linked their fingers. "A drink?" he asked as they entered the open space of the apartment.

"Am I allowed a glass of merlot?"

"You can have whatever you want." He released her hand and disarmed her with a smile.

"Alex?"

He hummed a syllable of consent as he

crossed to the wine refrigerator and selected a bottle of merlot.

"Maybe we should talk." She dropped her purse on the couch and approached the bar. "About the rules."

"Ah, the rules." He lifted a glass from the rack, popped the cork, and poured. "Rules aren't made to be broken." He handed her the glass. "But they can be negotiated."

She didn't want broken rules. She wanted to stay within the terms of their contract. She would be temporary in his life. Falling in love...and losing him would leave her shattered.

"I guess what I mean to ask"—she took a sip of the sweet wine—"is why are we here? You're teaching me about submission, but I know this isn't you. I've heard the whispers. I'm not your type. I'm not experienced." Insecurities had been building and seemed to bubble up all at once. "Don't make me fall in love with you."

Tears filled her eyes. She'd gone to the dungeon because love had left her damaged. Now, instead of setting her free, Alex seemed determined to pull her under again.

He crossed to her, took her glass, and set it on the bar. Then he was on her, his hands in her hair, his mouth on hers. Tongues touched and tempted. He overwhelmed her senses. Heat rushed through her. Her nipples tightened, and her pussy clenched.

A whimper escaped her. Powerless to

resist, she kissed him back. He held her firmly, crushing her against his chest. His hand roamed over her shoulders, and she slipped more under his spell. He tugged on the strap to her halter while his mouth roamed along her neck, kissing, tasting. Her head tilted to the side as his mouth blazed across her shoulders. Her dress loosened and slipped from her body to pool at her feet.

"Beautiful," he whispered. His knuckles brushed the hardened tip of her breast.

She shivered with the pleasure of his touch, knowing he would need more from her. He would want her submission. But those deliciously naughty delights took place in the dungeon.

Alex wrapped one arm around her back and the other under her knees and lifted her. She held onto his shoulders as he carried her to the west side of the apartment. He set her down on plush gray carpeting. Floor-to-ceiling windows stretched the length of the room and overlooked the city. His bedroom.

Dark woods for the dressers and wardrobes, deep red accent pillows and bedding, and black accents on the walls, and there was a king-size bed frame made of wrought Iron in the center of the room. Iron bars stretched toward the ceiling from each of the four corners and connected above to form a canopy. The iron and wood headboard was a St. Andrew's Cross, and the padded bench at the foot of the bed was placed ideally for bending her over and exposing her backside.

No, she wasn't ready for this. She took a step back, but he was there, his arm circling her shoulders as he kissed her neck. "Alex, we…we should be at Protocol. I don't belong here in your bedroom."

"Shh. You belong with me." His hand slipped lower. Her belly quivered as his touch floated across her skin. His fingers danced along the edge of her panties. "Do you trust me?"

"I do." She remembered his rules, wanted to meet his needs, but would he remember hers? She wasn't there for sex. She would keep reminding herself so she would keep believing it.

He dropped to his knees, hooked his thumbs into her panties and shimmied them down her thighs. He clutched the scrap of lace and silk into his palm, then stuffed it into his pocket as he stood.

"Don't worry, pet. We don't need to be at the dungeon to play." He crossed to a large wall armoire. The wooden doors opened. Inside, floggers, whips, and toys hung from the doors and shelves were full of ominous yet enticing leather cuffs, ropes, and spreaders.

In one hand, he held a collar and, in the other, a long sash of satin.

"When I mentioned something to put around your neck, I meant something like this." He fit the leather collar to her throat, fastening the links so a D-hook dangled at the base of her neck.

She swallowed, the weight creating a building tension within her.

He stared into her eyes, and his thumb grazed her cheek. He seemed ready to say something, but his jaw clenched. He took the sash and covered her eyes.

Evelyn pressed her fingers to her blindfolded eyes while he tied it behind her head. This was the first time he'd deprived her of her sight. Once tied, he led her to the edge of the bed. She ran her hands along the soft comforter, her thighs brushing the mattress. His bed.

"On the bed." His voice drifted away from her.

She hesitated. He wanted her in his bed. But she'd prefer to be on the bench or the cross. Intimacy happened in a bed. Sex happened in a bed. She'd fall in love in this bed. Her tummy tumbled, and her brain thought of ways to escape. *Patience. Patience. Patience.* Her mind screamed her safeword, but her body wanted on the bed where he wanted her. Indecision kept her immobile.

The quiet of the moment shattered. Music filled the room. Raw, industrial beats pounded through her, matching the rhythm of her heart. Strong, hard, and ferociously out of control.

"Evelyn." The way he said her name reminded her of her role. She turned and climbed onto the bed. "Thank you." The simple words pleased her. She wanted to please him. She just didn't want to love him.

The bed dipped. Each sound weaved into her mind, trying to visualize what would come next. Taking her hand, he strapped a cuff to one of her wrists and then he did the same with the other. Links of chain echoed in the room. Her arms hoisted above her head. She could kneel or sit, but she couldn't lie back.

"Take a breath," he whispered.

She inhaled and then gasped. A flash of pain streaked through her nipple as he pinched the tip in a clamp. Metal brushed her other nipple. She instinctively reared away from the pain. But his hand cupped the back of her head. He claimed her mouth, fiercely kissing her as the clamp bit down on her other nipple. Pleasure and pain mingled in her mind, overriding any lingering fears. He continued to kiss her, distracting her mind from the discomfort of the clamps, focusing instead on the dark possession of his kiss.

Finally, the initial pain numbed to a warming throb. She sighed and sat back on her haunches. He twisted the collar on her neck.

"Hold still."

She froze as he tugged on the D-ring. Links of chain clicked through the loop, and she felt the tug on her nipples as he connected the chain to the nipple clamps. Every move she made, every breath shifted the tautness of the chain and teased her nipples.

He chuckled, the sound an aural seduction, stripping her defenses.

"Alex?" She couldn't tell if he was still on the bed with her.

"I'm here." He wasn't on the bed. She couldn't tell how far away he was. Music drowned out any clue to what he was preparing to do to her. Anticipation rushed through her, teasing her senses. The darkness behind her eyes, the numbness in her arms and nipples, and the wetness between her legs heightened her senses.

She wanted to speak but had no words. She inhaled through her nose and blew out a slow breath, willing her nerves to settle and her heartbeat to calm. But the hard beat of the music wouldn't release her.

"On your knees." He pulled the chain on her arms, forcing her to rise to her knees. She sat too straight. The tether tugged her nipples. Erotic pain rippled through her breasts. She gasped and pitched slightly forward to release the tension on the chains linked to her nipples.

Leather tassels brushed the soles of her feet, not enough to tickle, but enough to make her smile. Gentle snaps flicked against her calves in a crisscrossing pattern. The falls didn't sting or hurt but revealed his intention.

She sank her teeth into her bottom lip, waiting for the sting, the blush of warmth across her buttocks. But the tassels teased across her inner thighs. She arched, suffering the tortuous delights on her nipples to feel the crack of the flogger on her ass.

Alex's hand curled around the globe of her buttocks. His finger traced the seam between her cheeks. She tensed, unsure of his target…unsure if she was ready for anal play.

She heard the flick of his wrist, just before the tassels barely snapped between her legs, just to tease but not sting. She cried out as her inner walls contracted and awareness streaked into her clitoris. Her arms instinctively yanked on the chains, and her hands curled around the links as another kiss of the flogger's tails struck her. Cream slicked her folds, and her core throbbed, aching for penetration. Penetration she wouldn't allow herself.

Alex was breaking down her resolve. The music hit a crescendo as the flogger snapped against her buttocks. Once. Twice. Her muscles quivered. Heat bloomed just beneath the surface.

"I'm not done with you yet."

She whimpered.

His mouth covered hers. She kissed him hard, taking all she could as her nipples ached, her arms grew numb, and her cream-slicked center pulsed, desperately aching for him.

The chains above her head loosened, but Alex's hands were on her before she could crash. She curled forward, relieving the pressure on her nipples.

"Lie back."

She reclined on her back. Fear, hot and potent, surged through her. Alex separated her arms, and the chains were repositioned, anchoring her to the upper corners of the bed. The chains on her nipples pulled taut again. She moaned. If she had use of her hands, she'd bury her fingers in her heat and release the pressure within her. She needed to come. She rode the edge of orgasm.

He gripped her leg. She bent her knee as he positioned her and strapped a manacle around her ankle. Then he did the same to her other ankle. Her thighs were spread, her body displayed to him.

Her chest tightened. She tried to draw in a breath, but her heart raced. She couldn't close her legs, couldn't push him away. Her safeword. She needed her safeword.

"Shh." His lips softly brushed hers. "Evelyn, say my name."

She gulped air. Her hands curled into fists. She couldn't speak. Her breaths came in hard sharp bursts. Fear coiled like a snake in her mind, ready to strike. She couldn't breathe. She couldn't see. The music drowned all thoughts. Darkness closed in on her mind. Panic welled within her.

"Evelyn," he said more forcefully. "Say my name."

"Alex," she choked.

"Again. Louder."

"Alex!" She felt as if she screamed, but the word barely slipped past her lips.

Alex ripped the blindfold from her eyes. She tried to focus in the dimly lit room. Alex hovered above her. He kissed her softly.

"Say it, and we stop." He kissed her eyes, her cheeks, then slid another kiss onto her lips. "Know your limits. Say your safeword."

Alex. Concern reflected in his dark eyes. His brows furrowed. While she'd been blindfolded, he'd stripped out of his shirt. Muscles bunched as he braced his weight on his arms.

Did she really want to fight her attraction? She teetered on the precipice of something elusive and freeing. She stared into his eyes, and her heartbeat slowed. Calm floated through her. She needed him. She trusted him. "Don't stop."

Alex growled and kissed her, a fast, hard, claiming kiss. Then he reared off the bed. He grabbed his riding crop, bending it between his hands as he approached the bed. Another wave of awareness washed over her. He'd popped the top button of his jeans, giving room for his erection. The shaft was hard and thick. Only the tip was exposed but held by the waistband of his black boxer briefs. Pearly essence glistened on the head. She licked her lips and swallowed.

Evelyn trembled at his nearness. He climbed onto the bed and leaned over her. His gaze softened. "Learn your limits. Your safeword only means play stops for tonight."

"The Professor said—"

"Say my name," he demanded. His eyes narrowed, and his jaw clenched. A vein in his temple pulsed.

"Alex."

"Remember who you belong to. Don't say another Dom's name while in my dungeon."

"Alex," she said again.

He slipped the clamp from her nipple. White hot pleasure-pain flashed through her nipple, raced along her spine, and settled in her pussy.

"Alex." Tears filled her eyes. The pain as intense as the pleasure. Her body shuddered.

He removed the second clamp. He flicked the red, distended nipple with the riding crop.

"Alex." She moaned. "Alex." The pleasure built too fast, the pain fading into a euphoric high. "Alex." She continued to whisper his name. "Alex."

Alex ground his erection into her heat. She rolled her hips. The music pumped through her. Emotions swirled in her head, but she couldn't focus, only feel. Her body tightened. He roared to his knees, slammed to the end of the bed, closed his mouth over her clit, and sucked hard. Slicing the blade of his tongue through her folds, he tunneled into her core.

She shattered—her heart and her body. She writhed beneath his mouth. She yanked the chains tight. Her legs tested the strength of the tethers.

Another surge of pleasure swept through her. He buried his face between her legs, tasting, licking, sucking her pussy. His fingers dug into her buttocks as he rolled his tongue through her juices.

Evelyn cried out. Uncontrollable quivering rattled her body. Alex held her tighter, kissing and tasting her until the last ripple of her orgasm ebbed. But he didn't penetrate her, not with his fingers, not with his cock. Because she hadn't asked. He honored his word. No sexual intercourse. She felt strangely hollow. She wanted to start the scene over, to give him the words he needed, to tell him her body was his, her heart was his.

He freed her legs. Then he kissed a path higher, grazing her belly with his lips. He laved her nipples, breathed against them, and with his lips, gently pinched and rolled the tender tips. With the tug on the buckle, he released her right arm and then her left.

And then he pulled her close and curled her into his body. Sweat slicked his skin. When she rested her head on his chest, his rampant heartbeat matched her own.

Evelyn realized it was too late. Too late to go back. And too late to deny her feelings. She belonged to him.

Chapter Ten

Alex padded barefoot into the kitchen. He wore his lounging pajamas but didn't want to dress. Evelyn still slept in his bed, where he could imagine having her every night, and he didn't want to disturb her.

The coffeemaker dinged. He grabbed his mug of French roast and went to the breakfast bar. He had his laptop open. Nash had emailed last night, and he'd left Alex a few unsettling voicemails. Apparently, if he didn't want to lose a fuck-ton of money, he needed to get his fucking ass to San Francisco because Nash wasn't able to clean up the fuck-fest of fuckery from fucking Frank Dunn. Alex smiled. When Nash was frustrated, his vocabulary reduced to one word. Fuck.

Nash had already called to have the jet on standby. He'd also sent Alex several emails with attachments to go over.

"Good morning." Evelyn stood just inside the kitchen…wearing his robe from the bathroom hook. She pushed her wild tangle of hair from her face. Her lips were just a touch swollen, and her eyes were sleepy. She looked like a woman who'd been fucked all night long. He wished she had been.

"Coffee?" he asked as he stood. He shifted

around the breakfast bar.

She crossed the kitchen. She seemed to hesitate, then she sat on the bar stool next to the one he had occupied. "Yes, please. Thank you."

He dropped a pod of French roast into the coffee machine. "How did you sleep?"

"I don't even remember falling asleep." She glanced down at her hands. "And when I just woke, for a moment I forgot where I was." She smiled. "But just for a moment."

"Do you want breakfast?"

She shook her head and wandered to the windows overlooking the city as the coffee brewed.

"I doubt I have any cream. But my housekeeper usually keeps milk in the fridge."

She returned to the breakfast bar, and he set the mug in front of her. "This is perfect."

"I have to go out of town today. I'm not sure for how long, but not more than a couple days."

"Oh. Then I won't see you. I, well, I can get some work done while you're gone. Plus, my sister is getting married, and she wants help with the wedding plans. And I promised my mom a scrabble match. So, it's okay. I'll keep busy while you're gone. I need to make some changes around my house, too."

She continued to rattle on a few more activities she could do while he was away.

"Will you call me when you return?" Her

brows pinched, and her eyes became glossy. She wouldn't look at him. "Or are you going to give me to someone else to train?"

Alex came around the breakfast bar. He cupped her cheek and, with a gentle nudge, forced her to look at him. "No. I won't call you when I return."

She audibly swallowed.

"Because I hope you will be with me."

"Oh." She blinked a few times.

"And no. Your training ended the first night at Protocol. You're mine…until you tell me you no longer want to be with me."

"Oh," she repeated, but this time she slowly smiled. "Then can I kiss you good morning?"

He kissed her, a brief meeting of lips. "A new rule." He tucked a tendril of her hair behind her ear. "I'll expect a kiss every morning."

She chuckled and lifted her coffee mug. "Well, that will be difficult unless you plan to cruise across town every morning." She took a sip. "You wouldn't expect me to drive over here every morning, would you?"

He'd explain the logistics later, after he convinced her to spend every night in his bed. Evelyn belonged in his private dungeon, in his bed, and in his life. "Will you fly to San Francisco with me?"

"Yes, Alex, I will. When do we leave?"

"In an hour. I need to make a few phone

calls. Then we can take off."

"I'll need to go home and pack a few things."

Right. He rarely took a bag to the Bay. He had everything he needed at his loft. "I'll make a few phone calls if you want to take a shower."

She stood and chewed her bottom lip. "Don't you need to take a shower?"

"Whatever you're thinking, it's a bad idea. I'm respecting your boundaries. I'm not strong enough to stand in a shower with you, wet, hot, and naked and not fuck you." He shifted his hand to the robe, slipped his palm between the folds, and grazed his fingers along her soft, warm flesh. "You do know how much I want to fuck you."

She swayed toward him.

"Go." Because his first time sliding into her heat, he wanted her tied up, a blush to her buttocks, her nipples red and swollen from his attention, and he wanted her writhing in pleasure. His cock kicked and his balls warmed. He swatted her bottom. "Take a shower. I'll call Nash and let him know our ETA."

***

Alex checked his watch. Evelyn had packed quickly at her house if he considered thirty minutes quick. He didn't. He still wanted to swing by the club and let Ronan know of his plans. Ronan handled the day-to-day operations, memberships, client issues, and any other potential complication that might arise.

Driving into the garage, Alex pulled into his spot. He grabbed his computer case. Joel or Ronan would drive them in the VIP vehicle to the regional airport where he kept the jet. "I'll just be a couple of minutes."

She nodded. "Do you want me to wait in the car?"

He chuckled. "I want you with me." He strode to the passenger door and opened it for her. Then he grabbed her small suitcase.

At the door, he punched in his code.

Inside, the club was quiet. A cleaning crew polished the doors, mopped floors, and cleaned the dungeon. Suppliers brought in stock for the bar and private rooms. The club also served a small menu of food items. "Do you want to wait in the bar? Chris is usually here early. He always has coffee."

She nodded. "I need to let Misty know where I'll be."

"What about your family?"

"No, I'll leave that to Misty. I don't want to have to answer a thousand questions."

He considered what he knew about her, what Nash had discovered, and what she'd revealed during their time together. He knew about her past employment, her education, and he knew she had resources, money in the bank from a life insurance policy payout. He knew about Daniel. "Will you tell your family about me?"

Her mouth smirked, and one eyebrow rose. "No." She shook her head. "Absolutely not."

The finality and strength in her refusal hit him like a punch to the gut. "Why?"

"What would I tell them? This is my...*friend*? My friend, Alex. I spend my evenings — and sometimes all night — chained up in his dungeons. But don't worry. We aren't dating. And no, I won't be dating anyone else, because I've signed a contract with him."

"When you put it that way, I wouldn't assume they'd approve." He stopped her and braced one hand against the wall. He leaned in close. She wore a long, cream-colored silk skirt and a light blue top. In the low cut of the neckline, her chest fluttered with her rapid breaths. He traced the V of her cleavage with the edge of his finger. "I'm much more than your friend, Evelyn. And even without the contract, we both know you're going to be mine."

Alex left her in the bar with Chris. He found Ronan in his office. "I shouldn't be gone more than a couple of days. Nash is meeting with the lawyers today." If the situation with Frank Dunn digressed, he might need more than a few days.

And there was Evelyn. Time away from Protocol, away from family, friends, and distractions might just give both of them a clearer understanding of whatever this was between them. Pleasure and punishment were part of the play, but there was a major component missing for him. A piece that had been missing for too long. He could fuck his fist until he was raw. It would never be enough. It wasn't sex. He wanted inside Evelyn, in her heart, her mind and in her body, with a need that bordered on desperation.

Twenty minutes later, they sat in the back of the luxury sedan. Ronan showed his credentials and drove into the private hangers at the regional airport. He pulled up to the jet, parked, and exited the vehicle. He popped the trunk as Alex pushed open the door, then held his hand out for Evelyn.

"Have a good trip, Boss." Ronan handed Evelyn's suitcase to him.

"Thanks. I'll let you know when we'll be back." He escorted Evelyn to the plane.

The wind whipped her hair around her face. She pulled the strands from her mouth. "I've never flown on a private jet."

They climbed the few steps into the plane. He couldn't remember the last time he'd flown commercial. His business took him all over the country. The small jet suited his needs. He'd had modifications done to the interior. Originally built for eight passengers, now there were four leather seats, plus a small sofa section and a desk and office chair.

"Good morning, Steve, Brian. Sorry for the late notice."

Captain Steve Anders laughed. "Nash

seemed a little tense when he called me at three this morning."

"I'm sure Linda was pleased," Brian, his co-captain, said.

"Pleased is the right word. Her sister is in town. Getting me out of the house fit well into her plans. Have a seat, Boss, and I'll get clearance for takeoff from the tower. Should be a nice flight. Good weather all the way."

Alex led Evelyn into the main cabin, dropped her bag in the galley closet, and set his laptop bag in one of the leather chairs.

Her brows furrowed. "Even your pilot calls you Boss."

"In this case, it's only because he works for me." He grinned.

He pre-checked the cabin. The private jet suited his needs. He didn't like people around him when he flew. Steve had been with him several years. Brian, he didn't know as well, but he was Steve's choice and Alex trusted Steve's judgment.

"Thank you," she said.

Alex glanced over his shoulder. "Thank you for what?"

"For inviting me along."

This was the first time since Siara that he'd invited a woman to travel with him. First time he'd wanted a woman outside of the dungeon. First time he'd wanted anything more than a pet in a playroom. First time he'd met a woman who touched on every trigger he had—he chuckled—and he hadn't fucked her.

"What's funny?" She sat on the small sofa and snapped on one of the seatbelts.

"Just thinking."

"About?"

He sat across from her. The engines revved, and the plane bumped along the tarmac. "I was just thinking about us, that I'm glad you're here."

She sighed heavily. "I wanted to talk about last night." She glanced out the window, then turned back to him. "You recognized I was losing it, that I was scared."

Her fear had been his fault. "You've never been sensory deprived before."

"No, but you've done a lot of things to me no one else has. I should have trusted you."

He leaned forward, resting his elbows on his knees, and stared hard into her eyes. "You trusted me to stop the scene. But you have to know the safeword is for a reason."

"I thought the safeword would end our contract."

The plane shook, the engines roared, and they lifted off. The plane glided higher. Alex sat back in the chair as the rush of takeoff tumbled through his stomach. Then he waited a few minutes for the noise to ebb. Finally, the wing dipped, and the plane leveled off.

"You can never be afraid to use your

safeword. If your Dom doesn't respect your limits, he's the wrong man for you. Where is the trust then? The only way to end our contract is for you to tell me you want out."

"I'm learning," she said. "I'll use my safeword." A shy smile curled her lips. "But only if I've reached my limit. I like being a little afraid of what you're going to do to me next."

When she said the words, his mind instantly conjured images best left for the dungeon. At the loft, perhaps in a drawer, he might have a set of handcuffs or a wooden spoon in the kitchen. But he didn't have a playroom, and there wouldn't be time to hit a club such as Salvage. At least not tonight.

"As soon as we land, we'll head to the loft. But Nash is expecting us."

"The loft?"

"My apartment." He crossed to one of the seats and pulled his laptop from the bag. Grabbing the back of the office chair, he spun it and sat. He turned toward the desk and popped open the computer. "I have a place in Kauai on the beach." He tapped a few keys and chatted to her while he pulled up his email. "But I don't get out to the island often."

"It just sits empty?" She unbuckled her seatbelt and curled her legs under her.

"Nash was there last month with Nadia." He glanced up. "You'll meet her tonight. She's making borscht, pelmeni, shashlik." He tried to make the words sound Russian the way Nadia pronounced them.

"She's Russian?"

"Ukrainian. But her parents are from Russia. They live in Seattle now."

"What about your family?"

"My father is an expatriate. He lives in South East Asia and, I'm sure, leaving a string of little Ferraro's in every country he visits. Growing up, my mother couldn't count on him. He served in the military, deployed around the world, but he was tough when he was around. Shit went south when he came home from the Philippines with a wife. Apparently, he'd forgotten he was already married. That sort of put the brakes on his marriage to my mother. He paid her off in the divorce. I was thirteen." He thought back to his first stepmom—there had been several more since—but the second Mitch Ferraro had left an impression...and a few scars on him.

"And your mom?"

"She died shortly after the divorce. I had to live with my dad." And this conversation wasn't going any further. A trip down memory lane only led to one place for him. Hell.

"I have a sister."

"Jane."

"Right." Her brows furrowed. "Have I mentioned her name before?"

"You must have." He couldn't remember if she had or not. But he knew from her file. A niggle of regret—more like guilt—wormed into his thoughts. Perhaps he should tell her about the information he had in her file.

"She's getting married next year. They are house hunting, have a wedding registry, and she's basically living DIY network. Only her version of do-it-yourself includes others doing the work or at least helping to do the work." She was quiet for a beat or two. "I haven't felt like doing...anything really, in a long time." Her gaze met his. "And then I found High Protocol."

She didn't have to explain the draw his dungeon had on her. He'd recognized her needs from her questionnaire. Since the first night seeing her with the Professor, he'd known she needed more than a scene in a private room. Like him, she wouldn't be truly content unless she lived the lifestyle.

"Come here." He spun his chair in her direction and patted his lap. "I need to touch you, and you need touched."

Evelyn shifted from her seat to his. He curled his fingers around the nape of her neck and pulled her lips to his. The first touch, a whisper of a kiss. Then with more pressure, he tempted her mouth to open, dared her tongue to tangle with his.

She sighed and surrendered.

Alex gripped her hips and shifted her, aligning the ridge of his erection with the soft swell of her buttocks. He ate at her mouth, revealing that his desire for her went far beyond the dungeon.

She moaned and broke the kiss. She drew in a ragged breath and rested her forehead against his. "I'm scared," she whispered.

"Of what? Of me?"

"Of wanting more than either one of us is ready for." She closed her eyes. "I'm being swept up into your world. But I'm not sure I want to be."

He clenched his jaw and willed his racing heart to slow. She had a better grasp on their situation they he did. She was right though. He needed to give her time to know what she wanted. Because once she was his, he'd never want to let her go.

Chapter Eleven

Evelyn assumed Alex had money when she'd met him at High Protocol the first time. He'd confirmed her suspicions when he picked her up in a hundred-thousand-dollar vehicle and taken her to his penthouse apartment. But the reality of his wealth hadn't really settled on her until he flew her across country on his private jet, put her in a limo, and had her driven to his loft. She'd mistakenly thought typical San Francisco real estate that she'd read about and seen portrayed in movies.

She'd been mistaken.

Although not as large as his penthouse, the loft was elegant. All white, chrome, and mirror. Not what she'd expect from her dark and dangerous Dom.

"This is beautiful," she said crossing to the wall of windows. A sliding door opened up to a balcony overlooking the bay. A cool salty breeze tickled her lips.

"The view sold me on the property." He set her suitcase down. "I'll give you the full tour tonight." He checked his watch. "Nash is expecting us, and it's getting late."

They'd picked up a few hours with the time difference, but clearly, whatever brought him to San Francisco on short notice took priority.

She checked her reflection in the mirror.

"You're beautiful," he said, coming up behind her.

She stared at their reflections. His dark hair next to her tawny brown tangles. Everything about him oozed mystery and seduction. His eyes seemed to see into her soul, and his mouth... Heat simmered just below the surface when she thought of the wicked pleasure in his kiss.

On the plane, he'd given her a glimpse into his soul. Had she not reveled in her own twisted needs, she might not understand Alex. But she did. He didn't have to say any more for her to accept his need for control. As a child he had none.

Once back in the limo, she thought of his business partner. Did he know Alex was a Dom, and if he did, would he assume she was his sub? Did he invite other pets to travel with him, meet his business partner, and eat borscht?

"Does Nash call you Boss?"

"Sometimes."

"Because he works for you?"

Alex chuckled. "Yes, but I see Nash as more of a business partner. I wouldn't make a decision without his input." He grabbed her hand and kissed her knuckles. "I should say I wouldn't make a *business* decision without his input." He glanced out the window. "We're here."

Nash lived in a rustic brick row house in the Presidio Heights neighborhood near Golden

Gate Park. A quiet, family community but still close to restaurants. A place to raise a family. A large bay window protruded from the front of the house. Ivy grew along the side of the door and over the window.

Alex held her hand as they exited the vehicle, then he placed his hand on her lower back as they walked up the dozen steps to the front door. He pressed the video buzzer.

"Fuck, about time," came the voice through the camera box. A moment later, the door flung open.

"I was here last week," Alex said and gave Nash a brotherly hug.

Nash smiled. "No, *I* saw you last week. And Nadia hasn't stopped reminding me about it."

"This is Evelyn Larsen."

Nash smiled awkwardly and then quickly turned his gaze back to Alex. Without giving her a chance to say hello, he immediately started talking business. Evelyn followed them both into the entryway. Stairs to the right led to the upper floor of the house. Nash and Alex walked straight through to the rear of the house.

For a few moments, she was a shadow, ignored and invisible, but expected to follow.

Nash paused in his nonstop chatter with Alex. "Did you want something to drink?"

Contract or not, she was going to need something stronger than water, because she didn't need to be psychic to see she wasn't going to be part of their conversation.

"Wine, beer, a shot of something. Anything really." So long as it took the edge off her nerves.

Alex stepped close to her. "Are you okay?"

"I'm fine, but perhaps I should get the driver to take me back to the loft. You have business to discuss, and you have enough to worry about without adding me to it."

"She'll have a glass of merlot," he called to Nash.

Squeals came from outside the door. "Ahlix," a woman who must be Nadia drawled as she came into the house. "You hurt my feelings you not coming to see me."

He kissed both of her cheeks. "It'll never happen again."

"Oh, you lie so beautiful." She turned to Evelyn. "I knew Ahlix find special woman." Nadia nodded to the back patio. "Meet Ava. Men need time for business. Bring wine," she hollered over her shoulder.

Unsure of how to respond, she followed Nadia outside. A ten-foot-high brick fence surrounded the outdoor living space. A rope swing hung from the framed-in awning. A raised hot tub filled the space on the left side of the porch. She walked down the four steps to a brick path the curved around a grouping of wicker furniture. The path continued to curve to a wooden activity playground. A little girl laughed as she chased a cat. Across from the furniture, there was a brick oven and outdoor kitchen area. And a fire danced in the circular stone gas fire pit in the center of the yard.

Nadia sat on the wicker lounger, tucked her feet beneath her, and smiled. Her blonde hair fell in a straight curtain around her shoulders. Big blue eyes sparkled as she stared at Evelyn. Red lipstick slicked her lips. She smiled. "Ahlix say you are beautiful. I never hear this from him before. He never talks about women, not about the club"—her voice grew louder as she spoke—"although I know he and Nash go to Salvage without me."

"Tell your wife not to spill my secrets," Alex said to Nash. He handed Evelyn a glass of wine and sat next to her on the couch.

"Ah dude, that ship has sailed. She doesn't listen to me anymore." He sat on the end of Nadia's lounge chair.

"I would still listen if you took me to club. But I'm mother and wife here. I'm not your kitty anymore when I have a child."

"She means, she's not my—" *Pussy.* He mouthed the last word. "I'm not allowed to use that word in the house any longer." He chuckled and lifted his beer toward Alex. "I have no power in my own home. She makes the rules."

Alex rested his arm along the back of the couch. His fingers brushed Evelyn's shoulder. She relaxed, leaning into him. He seemed comfortable, chatting with Nadia and Nash while he touched her, clearly demonstrating an outward show of affection for her.

From the conversation, she'd gleaned that at one time Nadia must have been Nash's submissive although those roles seemed to have blurred since parenthood. But both seemed to tease about it rather than fight against it.

Ava rode her tricycle along the brick path. She sang songs in Russian and jabbered in English. Nadia cooked in the outdoor kitchen while Alex and Nash discussed the problems with the leases on the building they were set to acquire.

Evelyn listened and sipped her wine. Alex talked but kept one hand on her thigh. "How many are new leases?"

Nash had his laptop open. "In the last week, he's renewed five, but in his initial proposal, he'd used original leases. Several of those have undisclosed addendums."

Evelyn shifted on the sofa.

Alex abruptly turned to her. "Everything okay?"

She smiled. "I need to use the restroom, and I thought I'd get a refill." She held up her empty glass. "Did you want a drink?" She'd never seen him drink alcohol, but the man consumed a vat of coffee, preferably French roast, every day.

"You get wine. I'll make coffee," Nadia

said, wiping her hands on a towel.

"Nadia, I'm sure Evelyn knows how to run a pod coffee maker," Nash said.

She gently smiled and returned to the outdoor kitchen. She said something to Ava in Russian, and the little girl skipped over to her playground.

Nash tilted his head to the door. "On the counter next to the refrigerator."

Alex absently ran his fingers along the back of Evelyn's thigh as she stood. He was once again engrossed with his conversation with Nash.

She found the restroom, then went to the kitchen. As the coffee brewed, she refilled her wine. Then she stood at the edge of the window. Alex listened as Nash spoke. He'd nod, then shake his head. Their voices occasionally grew louder, but not in anger with each other. Apparently, whatever decision they came to, the outcome was going to cost them capital.

Nash shifted his legs as Ava peddled her tricycle around the table. An ache settled in her chest. Nash and Nadia clearly had a D/s relationship. But Nash respected her, deferred to her decisions in matters of the home and family, but when he'd stopped her from making the coffee, Nadia hadn't questioned his interference.

Evelyn had foolishly thought that every Dominant and submissive were like the people she'd read about online or the individuals lurking in the chat room. She blinked before tears could fill her eyes. She'd wanted a life just like this…and then Daniel died.

Her gaze rested on Alex. And then she met this man. He'd changed her. He'd promised her he'd set her free. She closed her eyes and took a deep breath. She was deathly afraid he had… He'd set her free from her grief. Instead of dying, he had brought her back to life.

The gurgle of the coffee maker drew her attention. She took the drinks and rejoined him on the couch. She set the cup on the table.

"Thank you," he said to Evelyn and then continued to speak with Nash. "I'm not a fucking lawyer. That's why I keep them on retainer. And you're telling me none of them saw this coming?" He raked his fingers through his hair. "Un-fucking-believable." He shook his head. "Get me out of the deal."

"It's not that simple." Nash sighed and took a long drink of beer. "I don't see how I could have missed those leases."

"You didn't." Alex leaned back and rested his arm possessively across her lap again. "I guess we'll see what the damage is tomorrow."

"I don't profess to know about this particular situation," Evelyn said. "But there could be terminology in the contracts that afford you a way to mitigate your losses. I mean, if that is your endgame, it would be worth it to look."

"Our meetings are in the morning." Alex checked his watch. "I'm sure the lawyers have looked."

She shrugged. "Maybe, but they don't usually do the research. Their paralegals do. I mean, I used to be one." She raised a brow as she picked up her wine glass. "I can look at your contract. I might not find anything, but at least you'd know you had a second set of eyes on the documents." She grinned at Alex and took a hefty swallow. "You already know I'm not perfect with a confidentiality clause, but I recognized when I've broken one."

Nash laughed. "Yes, if you are offering, we are accepting."

"But not now." Alex's gaze darkened as it rested on her mouth as she took another sip. "Later. The files are on my laptop."

Keeping his attention on her mouth, she licked a drop of wine from the rim of the glass.

"I'm going to check with my wife on dinner." Nash stood and stepped away.

"You're playing with fire," he said, taking the glass from her fingers.

"Maybe. Or maybe I'm feeling warm from the wine."

He tipped the glass to his lips, finished the wine, then leaned into her. "You want another taste?"

She did…desperately. Crushing her mouth to his, she tasted the wine from his tongue. He groaned and slid his fingers into her hair.

"Oh, fuck," Nadia's thick accent sounded

nearby. "I think Ahlix is going to be trouble now."

Evelyn grinned through the kiss. "Are you trouble, Alex?"

"Yeah, I'm pretty sure I'm fucked."

"Maybe, but you'll have to take me home to find out."

***

Alex didn't drink. Either the half glass of wine...or Evelyn's invitation to take her home had his mind spinning. Nadia had spent the day cooking. Leaving early would be a dick move, but his mind wasn't on dinner.

Evelyn had another glass of wine. Nadia regaled her with tales of Nash and Alex. Her eyes glinted with mischief. When Evelyn laughed, his gut tightened, and his cock stirred. Until tonight, he'd never seen her truly enjoying herself. Sexual chemistry crackled between them. Everything she did flirted with his arousal—the flick of her hair, the pop of her bottom lip as she raked it with her teeth, and the lilt of her voice as she spoke his name.

"More coffee, Ahlix?" Nadia cleared dishes to the counter.

"I'm good." He didn't want more coffee. He wanted Evelyn. But she held Ava as the little girl fought falling asleep.

Nadia laughed. "No, you not good. I can tell you want to go."

Evelyn glanced over to him. "Are we

128

leaving?"

"Only if you're ready."

Nadia snorted. "Told you. Big trouble." She leaned over the table and collected a few more dishes. Nash spanked her backside. Nadia smiled but narrowed her eyes. "You want big trouble, too?" She sashayed her ass toward him.

Nash turned to Alex. "Get out."

Alex laughed and stood.

Nadia scooped Ava from Evelyn's arms. "Visit tomorrow?"

Evelyn glanced to Alex. "Whatever Alex wants to do is fine with me."

Nadia rolled her eyes. "Yes, you can go now. I don't need Nash reminded on how a good little kitty behaves."

Alex sent a quick text to the driver to let him know they were ready. He thought of the meetings in the morning with the lawyers and then with Frank Dunn and his attorneys. "Do you want to pick me up at the loft, meet there, or I can have the limo pick you up first?"

"I'll meet you there," Nash said.

Alex nodded.

Evelyn grabbed her purse.

Nash kissed both her cheeks. "I'll see you tomorrow, too."

The limo pulled up to the curb. The driver exited.

"I've got her," Alex said and opened the door for Evelyn. Then he climbed in after and pulled the door closed. Anticipation hummed between them.

"You seemed to enjoy yourself."

She smiled. "I did. They weren't what I expected."

He leaned back in the seat. "How so?"

"You said she was his submissive."

"She is."

"I expected a docile, obedient wife. I don't know, with a collar around her neck, led around on a leash."

"Nadia isn't the collar type. Nash will tell you she keeps his balls in her purse. But it's all teasing. They don't need reminders of their roles."

"Like us." Tension built in the small space. For a moment, she stared out the window, then her gaze met his.

"Like us?" He shifted to her side of the limo.

Her breaths came in sharp, little bursts. "I don't need a collar or a name to remember my role."

"I want more." He tugged on her skirt, bunching it over her knees as she sat on the seat.

"I know," she said on a breathy exhale.

Leaning in, he kissed her shoulder as his palm covered her knee. "No dungeon tonight." His fingers grazed the inside of her thigh. He kissed her on the tender skin at the base of her neck. "No playroom." His tongue flicked against her pulse. He curled his hand around her inner thigh and gently squeezed. "No safeword." His touch floated over her smooth skin.

Her eyes closed, and her head fell back against the seat. A moan escaped her lips. She shifted, opening her legs for him. Heat from her sex warmed his fingers. Wetness dampened her panties. He nudged the edge of the silk and lace to the side and slid his finger through her slick cream. "Fuck, Evelyn."

She turned her face, gripped his shoulders, and pressed her lips into his. She became the aggressor, demanding entrance to his mouth. Alex angled his body and claimed her tongue, and at the same time, he thrust two fingers into her silken passage. He slammed them deep into her, scissored them, pulled them back, and then slid into her again.

Her hand dropped between her legs, and she gripped his arm, urging him deeper and harder into her heat. But her panties kept him from feeling all of her sex.

"Take them off." He snagged the edge of the panties with his finger.

Evelyn lifted her hips, and he tugged the scrap of material down her legs and dropped them on the floor. He twisted her on the seat. She leaned back, her head toward the opposite door. Draping one of her legs over his shoulder, he spread her thighs. He leaned over her and crammed two fingers into her.

She cried out, her back bowing on the seat. He dropped to his knees on the floor, spread her wider and closed his mouth over her clit. He sucked hard, laving her folds with his tongue, then nipping her thighs as he fucked her with his fingers again. He built her up, pushing her closer to orgasm. Her fingers curled into the seat of the limo, white-knuckle gripping the edge.

"Oh god, I'm coming." Then her body tightened. Inner walls gloved to his fingers, pulsing and creaming. With a primal sexual cry, she shattered.

Alex licked, sucked, and fingered her while she rode the euphoric waves of release.

Evelyn was his kitty now.

Chapter Twelve

Alex held her hand and led her to the bedroom. He turned out the lights and opened the blinds to the windows. City lights twinkled in the foreground and outlined the bridge stretching across the bay.

She crossed the room and stared into the night. He shifted in behind her and kissed her neck. Neither spoke as he lifted her arms and pulled her top over her head.

"No games tonight," he whispered. "Just you and me."

"Will it be enough? Will I be enough for you?"

He turned her to face him, trailing his fingers along the side of her face. "You have no idea what you do to me."

She twisted his thoughts, made him want for more than he'd ever find in a dungeon. Not only did she need him to mask her emotional pain in the club, but a simmering sexual desire burned within her and the submissive in her had an innocent need to please. The Dom in him couldn't resist the lethal combination.

"I haven't been with anyone...not for a long time."

He smiled. "Good. I don't relish the thought of another man touching you."

"Alex." She rested her hands on his chest. "Is that the Boss talking or someone else? I don't know how to feel here. Am I a sub with a contract, or do you want something more? I mean, I know you want me, here, in your bed. But we won't be the same tomorrow if we do this tonight."

"I'll tear up the contract tomorrow." He didn't want her with him because of some twisted misconception about BDSM. "I want you. Tonight. Tomorrow. All of you. And yes, I want to fuck you in the dungeon because you're my submissive...and only mine. I won't share you. And I want you in my bed, all night, every night, so that I can make love to you." He narrowed his gaze and stared intently into her eyes. "Tell me now if that isn't what you want."

For a moment, he couldn't breathe. Fear ripped through him as he wondered if she'd pull away, tell him she wasn't ready for a fully committed D/s relationship, one that extended past the contract, the dungeons, and the expectations. He made his own rules. There was no formula for them. Nash and Nadia had navigated marriage, parenthood, business, and pleasure.

Alex could finally admit he wanted the same thing for himself. Perhaps not tonight, but he wanted to build something more obligatory trust with Evelyn. And he had to know it was him, not any guy with a flogger, taking her to subspace.

"I think I knew from the moment I first saw you behind your desk at Protocol. I was so afraid you'd be my instructor that first night because I couldn't imagine wanting anything more than to hurt and to be afraid."

Her soft, yet piercing eyes gazed into his. Her silken hair caressed his skin as he curled his hand around her neck.

"I can't pretend with you," she said. "I can't pretend you don't matter. I trust you, Alex." She fingered the hem of his Henley and tugged the fabric up his chest. He ripped it over his head. Her nails scored the line of his lats as she trailed them to the waistband of his jeans. She tugged the snap open and lowered the zipper. She stared into his eyes as she dropped to her knees and tugged his jeans just past his hips.

Hard, thick, and throbbing, his cock dropped forward into her hands. She caressed the length, sliding her hand over the taut skin. Leaning forward, she gripped the base with her right hand and curled her moist velvet tongue around the crown. Her left hand held his tightened balls and gently pulled and fondled the sac. Pleasure streaked along his spine and coiled in his gut, tighter and tighter. He squeezed his buttocks, urging her to take more of him into her hot, wet mouth. She sucked the head, pumping her fist and making mewling noises. He gripped her hair, holding her head, and relished in her decadent surrender. He slowed his breathing, willed his body to relax, to draw out the pleasure a moment longer.

Control was an issue for him. In bed, in business, and with himself. He clenched his jaw and staved off release. "I need you naked."

With the back of her hand, she wiped a bit of saliva from her mouth. She stood and shimmied her skirt past her hips. Reaching behind her back, she unhooked her bra and let it fall away from her body and drop to the ground.

Alex pushed his jeans down his legs and stepped out of them. He strode naked to the stereo and pressed a button. Rock music filled the room. He took her hand and led her to the bed. She climbed onto the mattress and lay back against the pillows. Hovering above her, he sliced his thigh between hers. He cupped her sex and slipped his finger inside her. Wet, hot, and slick with cream.

He growled and latched onto her nipple. He sucked and gently nipped the tip. He worshipped her body with touch and kiss. The music cocooned them in intimacy. He sipped at her lips, then dipped into for a deep scorching kiss.

Evelyn ran her palms over his shoulders. "Please," she begged, rolling her hips into his.

Understanding her desperation, because his need to be inside her bordered on pain. He leaned over to the nightstand, opened the top drawer, and took a condom from the dish. He reared up on his haunches, tore the package with his teeth, and stretched the rubber over his cock.

"Alex." His name on her lips should have dripped with passion and need. But her eyes filled with fear and uncertainty.

"What is it?" He combed a tendril of her hair from her eyes.

Her fingers braced his hips, and her thighs widened. She reached between them and curled her fingers around his cock, guiding him toward her entrance. "I know you're holding back." She moaned as the head of his cock breached her opening and slid inside her. "Make love to me later. Fuck me. Fuck me hard."

Alex chuckled, slowly withdrew, and slowly screwed back into her channel. She locked her legs around his hips and gripped his buttocks. He stilled.

Evelyn growled and nipped his shoulders.

He crooked an arm under her thigh, spread her wider, and pistoned hard into her core. She gasped as he pounded into her heat. Thrusting, nearly lifting her hips from the bed as he slammed into her again and again.

She panted, gripped the bed, and braced against the punishing onslaught of his prowess. Her body crested, then shattered. Quivers shuddered through her as she squeezed her eyes tightly closed.

But Alex hadn't finished his assault on her

senses. More than orgasmic, he wanted her spent and so thoroughly fucked she'd never want to leave his bed. He released her leg, bent, and kissed her trembling lips. He swept her mouth with his tongue, then trailed kisses along her neck, tickled her lobe, and whispered in her ear, "Just because I'm fucking you hard, doesn't mean we aren't making love."

Her eyes snapped open.

He reared back. "Roll over. I'm not done making love to you."

***

Evelyn flipped to her hands and knees. Her arms trembled, and she still sizzled with the fluttering pulses of her orgasm. Alex nudged her folds with his cock and slowly drilled into her. A whimper broke from her lips. He filled her, stretching her inner walls with his solid girth. Hot, hard, penetrating. He thrust deep until he couldn't press any further. His fingers held firmly to her hips, pumping into her heat. Harder. Deeper.

She reached for the edge of the headboard, holding tightly to it, and bracing her arm to keep her back bowed and rigid. He plunged unbelievably deeper. His cock grazed along the sensitive tissues, like a match to kindling, setting her on fire. She quivered. Her ass hiked higher, and her chest dropped to the bed. Both arms stretched over her head and braced against the headboard. Still, he continued his forceful drive in and out of her slick sheath.

Smack. His hand cracked against her ass, then slipped onto the curve of her hips and over her lower back. A bloom of heat warmed her buttocks.

Smack. Another burst of pleasure slicked her passage. He thrust his hips, faster, harder. *Smack.* The song on the stereo matched his motion. Drumbeats and pounding pleasure.

A tidal wave of energy surged through her. White light exploded behind her eyes. Her mind numbed. Volts of erotic heat centered in her clit. She'd never been wetter or come harder. Her body convulsed, her sex pulsing around his shaft.

Alex wrapped an arm around her, pulled her tight, crushing his groin to her ass and erupted with a shout. He locked her to him, muscles bunching and flexing as his body seized with his release. His chest, damp with sweat, pressed against her back.

For a moment, the only sound in the room was the harsh rasps of their breaths. Then the next song started on the stereo.

Alex sighed as he slipped from her body. He rolled to his side, taking her with him. Evelyn faced the windows. The city twinkled in the distance. Her body, replete in pleasure, settled into the bed.

He shifted behind her. She assumed he removed the condom, but she was too sated to move.

"Lift up," he whispered and kissed her shoulder.

She shifted her upper body as he pulled down the blankets. Then they tucked in under the covers. He spooned in close behind her, his front to her back, and draped an arm over her hips.

A tear slipped from her eye. He'd torn down the last of her resistance. She couldn't imagine being anywhere but in his arms.

A growl rumbled into her back. And then another.

"Are you asleep?" she asked.

Nothing...but another rumbling breath. She smiled and settled back against the warmth of his chest. Another new emotion welled within her. Contentment.

Evelyn must have fallen asleep. With slow even breaths, she listened to the silence in the room. Either the stereo had been on a timer or Alex had to have woken up at some point and turned it off. She carefully turned over. He slept on his back. One arm draped over his head. This was the first chance she'd had the opportunity to simply stare at the strong angle of his jaw and the soft curve of his slightly parted lips. Whiskers shadowed his cheeks. Thick brows and dark lashes framed his eyes.

She smiled.

And he snored a bit. A low rumble every couple of breaths, just enough to be charming in his sleep. She watched him for a few minutes, but then her restlessness had her stirring. Slipping from the bed, she quietly left the room, pulling the door almost closed. She'd need to turn on a light and didn't want to wake him.

In the living room, she found her suitcase. The zipper opening sounded loud in the room, but she doubted she'd wake him. She pulled on a pair of panties and a T-shirt, then went to the kitchen. The man had nothing in his refrigerator. Searching a few cupboards, she found a few packages of crackers from a fast-food restaurant and a box of French roast for the coffee maker.

In the dim light of the kitchen, she opened the package and ate a cracker. Outside, an occasional car's lights cut through the night. A neighbor's dog barked. Where she was…and who she was with settled over her like a warm blanket.

She glanced at the clock and sighed. Sleep would be nice. But she wasn't tired. Besides, Alex would be in meetings all day. There would be plenty of time for her to nap. She really should look at those files. She spied the laptop on the couch. Propping it up on the kitchen counter, she hit the power button and waited for it to load.

Please don't need a password for access. "Shit."

Of course, there was a password. She thought of Alex and something he might use. Dominant, submissive, High Protocol… She chuckled. Boss. But she couldn't see him using any of those words.

"Well, hell." How was she supposed to help if she couldn't access the computer?

Leaning forward, she looked at the keys. She could try something common. A lot of people used *password* as their password. A smile curled her lips. She typed French Roast into the bar and hit enter. The computer hummed to life.

Hmm. While the computer came online, she grabbed one of his pods and a mug and started the brew. The kitchen light buzzed. She wondered if he was a light sleeper because she seemed to be making a lot of noise.

Flicking off the light and using only the glow of the computer, she sat next to the windows overlooking the city and searched the laptop screen for the files.

His laptop was as organized and clutter free as the man. He didn't have knick knacks strewn around the house or pictures on shelves. A few expensive pieces of pottery sat on coffee tables, and framed prints hung on the walls. He was a minimalist. While there wasn't anything of the personal nature scattered about in his homes, there was only one space that revealed the man...his playroom.

Expecting a file that would say San Francisco or Frank something or other, something besides a series of numbers, she didn't see anything like that. All the files were coded. They could be dates, building numbers, file numbers. There had to be twenty folders on the screen. She started with the first file. This wasn't what she needed. The doc she opened listed a profit and loss spreadsheet for a mine in Kentucky. She opened two more, but she wasn't seeing anything that resembled leases or saved emails. Perhaps she really didn't know what she was looking for.

Clicking again, she opened a folder. Inside the digital file were several more files. Her gaze instantly locked on her name. A quick glance skimmed down the list. Siara, Delia, Elyse, Gwen, Gabi...

A sick feeling roiled in her stomach. There was only one reason her name would be listed with these women. Hoping these were nothing more than the questionnaires from High Protocol, she opened the top folder, Delia.

She pressed her fingers to her lips as she read the intimate details of another woman. A submissive woman. Custody disclosures for her children with two different men. Panic flashed through Evelyn. She hadn't considered that Alex might have children. She trusted him, had assumed he'd disclose something so significant.

Closing one file and opening another, she scanned Elyse, a young woman in college. Lived with her parents, but she had mental health issues. She'd been hospitalized. Evelyn closed the folder. Her heart hammered. This was none of her business. She should shut down the computer, climb back in bed, and pretend she hadn't seen this list. But her name was there, too. She swallowed, trying to dislodge the lump in her throat.

The folder with her name. The curser hovered over it. She clicked the button. The file opened. The taste of bile coated her tongue. She was going to throw up. Intense anger warred with agonizing hurt. Almost too difficult to believe. With the weight of a thousand lies, she realized the man she'd fallen in love with had betrayed her, used her, and deceived her into believing he cared. For what, to power over her? Fuck her? She'd been willing to sign a contract to let him do all of those things to her. But he'd taken more.

Everything about her was in the file. It wasn't the address, phone number, or even her likes and dislikes. He had her financials, her job history, notes on her family. Pain sliced through her heart. He knew about Daniel. Alex Ferraro knew everything about her...and she just realized she didn't know him at all.

Chapter Thirteen

Alex rolled to his side and stretched his arm along the bed. His eyes snapped open. Fuck, he couldn't remember the last time he'd slept so well. He smiled thinking of the reason why. The sheets were warm, and the bed still carried her scent. He breathed deeply, then swung his legs over the side of the bed, stretched, strode to the closet, and grabbed a pair of loungers.

Then he went to get his kiss good morning.

Evelyn sat quietly in the living room.

"Hi," he said.

She didn't speak. Fully dressed, shoes on, hair in a ponytail, she rested her hands on her knees. Quickly scanning the room, he assessed the situation. Her suitcase waited by the door, along with her purse. His laptop was on the counter, but the screen was dark. Evelyn wouldn't look at him. She was leaving. But after last night, why?

"What's wrong?" He leaned against the wall and crossed his arms over his chest. He projected calm, but inside, emotions boiled.

"Because I was wrong. This isn't what I want—" She finally turned and glared at him. "— and you aren't what I need." Her brows pinched.

He took two steps toward her, but she stood and put up her hand. "Don't. I've called a ride share. They'll be here in a minute."

Tightness choked him, fear squeezing his chest. "Don't do this. Talk to me."

She shook her head. Tears filled her eyes, and her lips trembled.

"Please, Evelyn. Say something to me."

She closed her eyes and took a slow long breath. Then she met his gaze and whispered, "Patience."

The simple word nearly took him to his knees. She crossed to the door and rested her hand on the handle. "Goodbye, Alex." She picked up her suitcase.

He rushed across the room and slammed his hand against the door. "This is my fault. I pushed you last night. We can slow down. Fuck, you said your safeword. This scene ends. Don't go. Please." He whispered the last word. A plea for her to stay.

Her back stiffened. "I have to." She glanced over her shoulder to him. Tears swam in her eyes. "You know who I am." She blinked, and the tears spilled onto her cheeks. "But you aren't who I thought you were. Last night, you said you would tear up the contract. You should." She released a breath and whispered the words he'd told her would end their association. "I want out."

She spun away, yanked open the door, and rushed out.

Alex couldn't move. What the fuck had he

done?

No. No. Pain ripped through him. His heart ached and his mind numbed with disbelief. No. She wasn't leaving. Fuck that. Oh god. Fuck him. He couldn't lose her.

He threw open the door and went after her. He ran down the stairs and out onto the street. "Evelyn," he hollered. Fuck. Fuck. Fuck! He burst through the door to the street and stubbed his toe on the concrete. "Evelyn!"

She closed the door to the ride share, and the vehicle pulled away from the curb. He ran after it, but he was too late. She was gone. She'd left him.

What the fuck? He ran his fingers through his hair. His gut churned and his heart ached. Not one for crying, he felt the burn of emotion filling his eyes. He squinted against the morning sun, took a settling breath, and returned to the loft. Once inside, he leaned against the door.

His hurt began to morph into something more dangerous. Determination. She wanted out? Fine. But she was going to tell him why.

He strode to the bathroom, stripped out of his pajama bottoms, and turned on the shower. Last week, he'd been almost content...in his dungeon, at work, with his friends. Now, he didn't even want to touch his own dick. He only wanted Evelyn.

Thoughts tumbled through his mind. He had no idea where she'd gone. All he wanted to do was go after her, but he had to talk to the lawyers. His attention would not be on the meetings. The city had her charm but also a dark side. Perhaps that was the appeal. One could say he shared similar traits.

After he dressed, he called for the limo. Nash sent a text. *On my way.*

Thoughts twisted in his head. He couldn't focus. Now, he was running late. As he bumped his laptop to close it, the screen blinked. Breath rushed from his lungs with understanding of the situation. Evelyn had logged onto his computer. Nash had told her to go over the leases. Alex had agreed. Sometime this morning, she'd done exactly what she'd been told to do. And found his personal files. He slammed his fist to the counter. Of course, she'd be pissed. He'd violated her privacy.

He snapped the laptop closed, shoved it into its case, and left the apartment. As the limo drove him to the meeting, he considered the ramifications of what he'd done. Not that he would have ever told her, but since she did discover the file, he would have explained why he'd had Nash dig into her life. He'd needed to know her history…but he should have shared his.

The limo stopped. Alex bent to grab his computer case and noticed the hint of lace and satin under the seat. Evelyn's panties from last night. He clutched them in his fist, praying he hadn't lost the woman…the submissive, he'd been waiting for.

Nash waited on the sidewalk outside the offices of Kingsley and Everett. "Christ, do you think you could be on time on the day we stand to lose...what? Two million dollars?"

Alex strode to the brass and glass doors. "I don't care about the money."

Nash's eyes widened. "You might not, but I fucking do."

They stalked to the elevators.

"Evelyn left."

Nash glanced to Alex as he pushed the up button. "She went home?"

Alex clenched his jaw and shrugged. "Maybe. She called a ride share and took off." Just saying the words had his heart pounding and pressure building behind his eyes. "Or maybe she found another place to stay here in the city. Or went on another one of her internet searches for another Dom. Fuck, if I know."

But he knew everything else about her...because he never let anyone close.

The elevator doors opened. "Alex, what happened?"

"We told her to go over the leases."

"Good" Nash nodded. "Did she find a way out?"

Alex swallowed the lump in his throat. "She did. She found my files." He turned to Nash. "My personal files."

Nash leaned back against the wall of the

elevator. "Did you explain?"

"Didn't get the chance. And we both know there is no explanation." He'd lost count on the number of times Nash had cautioned him, warning him that there were some things he didn't need to know. "She said she wanted out." The doors opened. Alex took a step forward. "But I can't let her go."

***

Throughout the morning, the lawyers went back and forth with Nash. Alex sat at the table and listened, but his thoughts were on Evelyn. He checked his phone again. No text, no calls. He sent her another text.

—I know why you're upset. I can explain. —

But could he? She'd come into High Protocol with specific needs and contracted for specific training. Where in that arrangement did he get the right to alter the terms?

"Alex?"

He glanced up from the phone. "Sorry, what was that?"

"We need to know what you want to do."

He wanted to get out of this meeting, get in the car, find Evelyn, and plead for another chance. The tough, no-emotion Dom wanted on his knees, begging her forgiveness. He wanted her to trust him, more than he ever allowed himself to trust her.

"The longest lease is ten years," Nash said.

He didn't care.

"The tenant could sue, and they'd have legal grounds."

He didn't care.

"Bottom line, how much are you willing to lose and how committed are you to the deal?"

He didn't care...about the money, about the deal, or about the fucking leases. He could care once he knew Evelyn was safe.

He sighed and leaned back in the chair. Add stubborn to her list of qualities. He wanted a submissive partner, but he also wanted a woman with personal fortitude. That she would make him earn her surrender only made her more perfect for him. But until she called or sent him a text, he couldn't tell her, couldn't show her what she meant to him. And she wouldn't answer.

Alex needed his head in the negotiations. Someone needed to pay for his frustration. It might as well be Frank Dunn.

They worked through lunch, ironing out where they were willing to find concessions. As Alex listened to his lawyers, he realized there had to be compromise in any negotiations. Including in love.

By late afternoon, they had their counteroffer prepared for Frank and the lease holders. If they declined, the loss would sting for Alex and his associates, but Frank would be reckless with his solvency if he turned it down. Alex was prepared to walk away from the table. This was business.

However, Evelyn was personal, and he couldn't let her go. Not without a fight.

"Come over," Nash said as they parted with the lawyers. "Nadia has dinner started. Let her feed you. It'll make her happy."

Alex laughed. "And listen to her catalog my faults?" He shook his head. "Tell her I'll see her later."

There was a moment of silence between them. "Alex, you can't force her. If she wants out, you have to let her go."

Chills broke along his arms. "I know."

But he didn't believe she truly wanted out. She was just hurt...betrayed. He knew how that felt. He'd been there before.

The limo pulled up to the curb.

"Alex, if you need me to handle the meeting tomorrow, I will. We're down to a yes or no." Nash opened the rear door of the limo before the driver could exit the vehicle. He put his hand on Alex's shoulder. "And call me when you find her."

Alex nodded as he climbed into the limo.

"Sir?" The driver awaited their destination.

"Home." Maybe she'd be there.

However, once at the loft, he was greeted with cold emptiness. He dropped his laptop on the couch and sat in the quiet. Waiting. He checked his phone for the hundredth time. Inside, he was going crazy. Outside, dusk blazed a golden reflection off the water in the distance. Car horns beeped, and a police siren cut through the silence. With each minute, tension built. He had no idea where to look for her.

Maybe she had gone home. As far as he knew, guilt tore through him because he did know, she didn't have family or friends in San Francisco.

Sitting on the couch, he pulled up his contact list and found the name Misty Kemp. Shit. She was on the East coast. Two hours ahead, but he'd guess Misty wasn't the type to be in bed early.

"Hello, Alex."

From the tone of her voice, he didn't need to ask, but he did anyway. "Have you heard from her?"

"No. And you're an ass." She puffed a sigh into the phone.

"How would you know I'm an ass if you haven't heard from her?"

"Because I do what I'm told." She made a sound between a grunt and a snort. "Maybe not to your definition of obedience. But to quote, 'If that asshole calls, tell him you haven't heard from me.' And then she told me everything. And I agree with her. You are an ass."

He leaned forward. Holding the phone to his ear with one hand, he covered his eyes with the other. A couple of silent tears leaked through his lashes.

"Alex?"

He sniffed, straightened his shoulders, and blinked a few times. "Yeah," he managed to say. Knowing she'd called Misty, eased his burden a bit. "Is she there or on her way home?"

"No. She's staying at a place in North Beach. Do you know the area?"

Hairs prickled on the back of his neck. "I do."

"Alex, she's hurt."

"I know. I made a mistake." The mistake was in not telling her.

"Maybe in your research on her you learned a few things, but I doubt you know everything. I won't betray her, but she found you because of the damage losing Daniel did to her."

He'd read the newspaper article. Daniel had died in a car crash. Evelyn had been driving. But the report had indicated the accident occurred in bad weather. Ice had built up on the roads. Speed nor alcohol had been a factor. Just a tragic sequence of events.

"She came to your club because she needed a place to put the hurt. Now, you hurt her. That's why I'm telling you this. For the last hour, I've been in a debate with myself. If you hurt her again, I swear I'll come there and take a whip to your ass. Evelyn might enjoy that, but you won't. Not the way I'll thrash the fuck out of you."

He loved her defensiveness of Evelyn. "Where is she?"

Damaged

"She found a place in San Francisco. Have you heard of a place called Salvage?"

Chapter Fourteen

Salvage was nothing like the elegant opulence of High Protocol. Evelyn tried to appear calm, but inside, fear had her in its clutches. Unlike the uncertainty she felt those first moments with Alex and the Professor, she wondered if she'd made a colossal misjudgment.

Several people milled about. Men had their slaves in collars. A woman in a cat suit walked her sub, a man in a latex hood, on a leash. Salvage played at a higher level of kink than she'd seen before. This was Alex's world. Salvage could be hers as well.

She'd spoken to Master Flint, and because she'd wanted Alex to share in the responsibility of her being her, she'd used his name to gain access. She hadn't been sure they would even recognize the name. That they did hurt even more. Not that she had a right to his history. Another wave of anger washed over her. Just as he had no right to hers.

"Patience?"

She turned at the name...the name she'd chosen as her dungeon name. She didn't need a safeword. She'd believed she was safe with Alex, both emotionally and physically. He'd had all the tools—her life, her history, her love—to manipulate her.

"Do you want a drink?" The man in leather chaps and a leather chest harness put his hand on her back.

Patience. She had to remember her role and not pull away from his touch. Uncomfortable quivers flitted through her, tumbling her tummy and making her heart race. She shyly looked to her bare feet, the way her Dom requested. She'd agreed to a scene with Lord Jovan. She'd call him Lord or Lord J as he didn't allow his subs to use his full name. She'd been given the safeword of red and a warning word of yellow if she was growing uncomfortable with the play.

Lord J led her to the bar. The dungeon was dark and erotic. Red lights pulsed. Music set the tempo of the room.

"Two waters," he said to the bartender and then turned to her. "My rules."

"Water is perfect." She took the bottle. "Thank you."

He took a drink of his water, but his stare never left her face.

"Is something wrong?" He was making her uncomfortable.

"I'm not sure yet. But something feels off." He leaned against the counter. "How long have you been in the scene?"

She furrowed her brows. Why couldn't he just strap her to a bench and warm her with a flogger. She didn't want to know him...and she didn't want him to really know her. "Not long."

He nodded. "Then what is the deal with Alex, I mean the Boss? He doesn't keep pets here at Salvage, especially inexperienced ones."

"I never said I was one if his pets. And I never said I was inexperienced."

He leaned in and spoke near her ear. "Experienced submissives don't challenge their Doms. I tell you when to speak, what to feel, and when to come."

She nodded. "Yes, Lord J?"

She could do this, prove to herself that she could respond to another Dom, that she hadn't responded to Alex because of something more. She hadn't fallen in love with him.

"Take off your panties."

Her gaze darted around the room. Here? Panic, hard and swift surged within her.

"Patience, take off your panties."

Evelyn slid off the chair. She'd worn a short black skirt and a black bra with a red tank top. Reaching under her skirt, she grabbed the edge of her panties and pulled them down her thighs. She wiggled until they slipped past her knees and pooled at her feet. Careful not to expose her ass, she squatted and picked them up.

"Hand them to me," he said. She did, and he rubbed the crotch between his thumb and finger. "I'm disappointed. I want you wet. Master Flint said no intercourse." He brought the panties to his nose.

"No."

His gaze narrowed.

"Lord J, no sex. Oral or intercourse."

"Ah, you don't want fucked or sucked." He took her hand. "But I want you begging for cock."

This was wrong. She didn't belong here. She didn't belong with Alex either. Her stomach roiled. Maybe she did belong with him...or maybe she belonged *to* him.

Indecision warred within her head. She could yank her hand free, run from the dungeon, and return to her dark, depressed life alone. Or she could take this last punishment. Find the strength to retake her power through submission. The Professor had shown her that she wanted this. She could have it without love. She wanted to be free.

Lord J led her to a semiprivate room. The room was typical of what she'd seen online. It wasn't warm and sexual like Alex's bedroom. Nor was it High Protocol. Good. She didn't need reminded of what she wanted. This, Lord J, and a group dungeon was what she could have.

Her choice. Her scene. Her decision.

Then why did this feel like betrayal? She closed her eyes as Lord J kissed each of her fingers. "Look at me, Patience."

She focused on his face. But he didn't have a beautiful strong jaw or dark lashes and brows. His lips didn't hint at a smile as he encased her wrists in steel manacles.

Methodical and practiced, he stretched her arms over her head. The motion hiked up her skirt, exposing the cheeks of her butt and hinting at the mound of her sex. She didn't feel empowered or free. Humiliation suffocated her. She wasn't a pet for a dungeon. Alex had awakened her. She closed her eyes as the first thrash of the flogger broke along her backside.

Lord J didn't tease her into a frenzied state of arousal. He gave her what he believed she wanted. Bondage, heightened awareness of her sexuality, submission to a power outside of herself to bring acceptance inside. She felt none of those things with the stinging whips.

"Patience," she whispered to remind herself this was her role. "Patience." Tears filled her eyes, wishing her life could be different. Wishing for more. She wanted Alex, the trust, the erotic bedroom, the sensual kiss of his straps. A flogger struck her again. "Patience."

***

Alex stood in the back of the room. Pain knifed through him. Evelyn's eyes were closed, reveling in the pleasure of another Dom. He wielded his flogger, coloring her beautiful ass with a becoming blush of crimson. He could imagine how wet she was getting. Those sexual little mewling sounds she made as she fought against her arousal.

Those perfectly straight teeth sank into her bottom lip. She flinched against the snaps of the tassels. Her full, luscious lips, the same ones she'd wrapped around his cock, pouted with the pleasing pain. She whispered. Breath caressed her lips. He could imagine it on his.

His gaze narrowed. She whispered again. Her lips moved in a continuous motion. White-hot anger surged through him. His hands curled into fists. He shoved his way through a couple of people and roared into the scene. "Don't fucking strike her again."

The Dom dropped his arm.

Evelyn's eyes snapped open. "Alex." She said his name like a plea. Tears filled her eyes and slipped onto her cheeks.

"I know you," the Dom said.

"I don't know you. But I know her. Don't you fucking listen?" He shoved the Dom away and unhooked her arms from the rigging. "She said her safeword three fucking times!"

"Get out of here. We just got started, and she didn't say shit. Except not to fuck her."

Evelyn's arms dropped in front of her. Alex unhooked the clasp and removed the manacles.

He turned to stand equal with the guy. The Dom might outweigh him by twenty pounds, but tonight it wouldn't matter. He'd lay the guy out if he put a fingertip on Evelyn.

"Patience, I didn't hear yellow or red." He spoke to Evelyn.

"I didn't use the safeword, Lord J."

Alex paused. Patience? He glanced to Evelyn. "Why is he calling you Patience?"

Her eyes filled with tears again. "Because I don't need a safeword. You taught me that. I need a dungeon name to remember my role."

The broken look in her eyes crashed through what was left of his anger. He wrapped an arm around her shoulders and pulled her close. She leaned into him, gripping the front of his T-shirt. Her body shook with tears.

"Can I take you somewhere?" he asked her. "To talk."

She nodded against his shirt. "I'm sorry."

"You don't have anything to be sorry about." He pressed a kiss to her temple. "This is my fault. All of it."

Alex turned to the Dom, the one she called Lord J. "Sorry about this. I misunderstood the scene." He tightened his hold on her. "And so did she." He locked gazes with him. "She's mine."

The man nodded. "Understood."

Alex kept her close as they made their way out of the club. The limo waited at the curb. Opening the door, she climbed inside. He couldn't help but smile at the peek of her ass, but hated that the blush to her cheeks was put there by someone else. He climbed in after her. She sat on the seat...and stared straight at him.

"Where are your panties?" he asked.

"I gave them to Lord J. He asked for them."

"For future reference, you aren't to give your panties to anyone except me."

She cocked her head to the side. "More rules."

"Oh, yes, we're going through the whole fucking textbook tonight."

Her brows furrowed. "Two minutes ago, you were comforting me and saying we need to talk."

"Come sit on my lap."

"No." Her mouth pulled into a tight line. "Stop the vehicle and let me out."

He chuckled. "Not in that outfit. Who dressed you?"

"None of your business. And you know what else isn't your business? My family. My friends. My financials. And sorry, but any one I've slept with in the past, present, and future is also none of your business."

"Present and future are definitely my business. We can debate the rest." And he'd win the argument.

She swiped a tear from her cheek. "Daniel certainly isn't any of your business."

Alex hated that he'd hurt her. He could offer an explanation. Although that didn't change who he was or that he'd do it again. "I was twenty-two when I started my business. Nash and I were at Harvard together. We enjoyed the same extra-curricular activities. He played in the dungeons. I met Siara." Alex remembered back to those early years. He'd been naïve. "I played at being a Dom. I wouldn't say I was one. But Siara was submissive."

His gaze met Evelyn's. She no longer had her hands fisted at her side. She leaned back on the seat, listening intently to him.

"I work a lot. Then and now. While I was building an empire, I believed her when she said she was planning our future. I bought my first building. She took her first lover. I moved us into the penthouse. She moved onto another Dom." He smiled. "And no, not the same penthouse."

"Were you married?" She licked her lips.

"No. Trust, loyalty…love. Those words didn't mean anything to her. She wanted something different than I did. She found someone…anyone who would choke her out, spit on her, rape play. I'm not into that scene."

"I read about those things online."

"She sued me for breach of contract. She would have destroyed my business and my reputation. I paid her off and opened High Protocol."

Her lips twisted in a skeptical smirk. "You opened your own dungeon so you could have sex with subs and avoid any future psycho ex-girlfriends."

"I had no plans of ever having future ex-girlfriends." He couldn't help the smile on his lips. "I still don't." He hoped she understood he had no intentions of letting her go once he'd become involved. "I have Nash do a background check on any woman who could potentially enter my personal space. I don't take unnecessary risks." His gaze drilled into her. "Ever."

"Is that supposed to make me feel better? What was wrong with Delia, Gwen, Mary, Jennie or Judy or whatever their names were in those folders? Did they not scream loud enough? Were they too meek or maybe too bossy? This one preferred spankings, and you prefer a flogger?"

He leaned back in his seat. "Is that what you think? That the women in those files were all subs in my past?"

"Yes," she stated. "That's exactly what I think." She growled and raked her fingers through her hair. "You piss me off."

"I think you're hot when you're pissed. I love a challenge."

"I'm not a challenge, and you're not turning this around. You had no right to dig into my past."

"You're right. But I did. If I hadn't, you and I would never have happened." Her skirt skimmed the top of her thighs. "Spread your legs."

"Absolutely not." She snapped her thighs together.

"Delia is the manager of a property in South Florida. I needed someone I could trust, and she needed out of town. Her ex made life rough for her and her kids."

"Oh." She seemed to weigh his answer in her mind. He could almost see her thoughts coming together in the tilt of her mouth and the arch of her brow. "And Gwen?"

He leaned forward. "I'll tell you anything you want to know. But you have to do what I say without questioning or arguing."

Her gaze narrowed. "Anything I ask?"

"Anything."

"I'm first. What about Gwen?"

"Spread your legs." His heartbeat spiked as she slowly spread her legs. He used his hands to indicate he wanted to see more of her secrets. The flounce of her skirt still covered her. "Lift up your skirt."

She cocked a brow.

"Gwen applied to clean my house. I wasn't comfortable with what I discovered in her history."

"Did you hire her?"

"Lift up your skirt."

She pulled up her skirt, exposing the soft petals of her sex.

"No. I called in a favor with a friend." He shifted his gaze from between her legs to her face. "She has a franchise with a maid service. As far as I know she still works there."

"I wasn't applying for a job."

"Is there a question in there because I need you to touch yourself?" He reached into his jeans and adjusted his cock.

"Why did you do a background check on me?"

He was quiet until she slipped her fingers between her folds and rubbed the edge of her clit. She leaned back on the seat, opening wider, and smeared her juices with her fingertip. "Alex, why the background check?"

"Because I didn't want to risk getting involved with someone with...complicated baggage." He groaned as her fingers slid inside her passage.

"Do you do a background check on all the submissives you get involved with?"

"Take off your shirt and bra."

She smirked. "That's two things."

He clenched his hands into fists. "Then ask two questions." His words were clipped. Pressure built in his balls as they tightened to his body.

She lifted off her tank top and set it on the seat.

"No, I've never done a background check on a submissive in the club."

She paused. "I didn't ask about the club. What about your submissives?"

He twirled his finger to show the bra needed to come off first. She reached behind her back and unhooked the bra. She sat on the seat, naked except the skirt bunched around her waist.

"I don't have relationships with submissives. I play in the dungeons."

"Do you sleep with them?"

"Sit on my lap."

She hesitated. Her eyes widened in the dimly lit interior. He gave her time to make her decision. Did she want to know the answers to her questions or to end the game here? She shifted and crossed to his side of the seat. She braced her thighs on the outside of his and settled on his erection. She bit back a moan as she rode the edge.

"Do you sleep with the subs at the club?" she repeated as she rested her hands on his shoulders.

"Do you want to know if I sleep with them...or if I fuck them? Because I haven't slept in a bed with a woman since Siara. Until you."

"Do you fuck the subs in the dungeon? And it's the same question so I've already paid for the answer."

"Yes, I fuck them."

"When was the last time?"

He clenched his buttocks, pressing his cock into her heat. "Before you?"

She rolled her eyes. "Yes, I remember the last time you fucked me."

He laughed and gripped her hips, anchoring her to his groin. "A few weeks ago. Before you sent in your questionnaire to High Protocol."

"You aren't sorry for invading my privacy."

"No. But I should have told you. And I

should have been honest with you about my past. Now pinch your nipples."

"Why? I didn't ask a question. I made an observation. You aren't sorry."

"You're right. I'm not. Because I won't regret our relationship. Now ask a question?"

She stared hard into his eyes. "Have you slept with Nadia?"

He paused. The question surprised him...and bothered him. "No." He wasn't going to exchange the answer for titillation. "Never."

"Do you want to?"

He leaned up. "Evelyn, ask me if I want what Nash has?"

"I just did. Do you want Nadia?"

"You want the answer?" He banded his arms around her. "Kiss me."

She stared wildly into his eyes. She tried to brush a kiss to his lips, but he forced her mouth open with his, slicing his tongue into her mouth and tasting her. She whimpered and kissed him back. He angled his head, crushing his mouth to hers. "No. I don't want Nadia. And don't pretend you don't know what I mean."

She rested her hands on his cheeks. "Do you want what Nash has?" Tears leaked from the corners of her eyes. "Do you want a submissive?" She gulped a breath. "Do you want a submissive for a wife? Children?"

His hands roamed up her naked back, trekking along the ladder of her spine. "Yes. One day. I want to share my life with you. I want to fall in love. I want you bound to my bed...but I also want you on my arm. Every day. I don't want to wonder if you are all in. I want to trust in us."

Evelyn rolled her hips. "Do you want to make love to me?" She reached between their bodies and traced the ridge of his erection through his jeans.

"Touch my cock."

She rose onto her knees, still straddling his lap and reached into his jeans. Her warm fingers curled around the length. "Answer my question."

"Yes, I want to make love to you." He shoved his jeans past his hips. "Please ask another question." He was desperate to settle her over his lap and bury his cock in her heat.

"I don't think sex in a limo can be considered making love." She braced one hand on his shoulder and the other on the headliner of the vehicle.

"Evelyn." He couldn't wait another moment. He gripped her hips and thrust into her. She gasped as she settled on his lap, taking his cock into her hot, wet core.

She moaned and rocked on his lap. "One more question."

"Yes. Whatever it is, yes. Whatever you want? Yes."

"Puurfect. When we get home, will you show me how a good little kitty should behave?"

Damaged

Chapter Fifteen

Evelyn's pulse pounded to the music. The scent of sandalwood and sex lingered in the room...Alex's room. She moaned as hot, wet kisses trailed across her quivering belly. Teeth nipped at her flesh. The blindfold robbed her of sight, but she felt every dip of the bed, heard the music, the shift in his breath as he teased and punished her body with decadent pleasures.

She moaned as he sucked her warm throbbing nipple. Straps from the corner of the bed banded around her ankles and kept her legs open. Although she couldn't see, she had use of her hands. Alex hovered over her, worshipping her body with his mouth and hands. His hips teased the inside of her thighs. She wanted to lock her legs around him as he rode her hard and fast, but she had to endure the sweet torture of his slow build.

"Are you still wearing my ring?" She reached between them and curled her fingers around his thick, hard shaft. A tight latex ring circled the base.

He growled. And she chuckled. She braced her feet against the bed and rolled her hips. She needed him inside her. "Alex."

Shifting his positioned, he settled between her thighs, and she guided him into her aching core. He sank into her, a guttural moan of completion rumbling from him. He reared back and thrust hard into her again. And again. She braced her hands over her head against the headboard. He gripped her hips and lifted. The straps on her legs jerked taut. Cream slicked her passage. Shivers raced along her spine. Shards of light flashed behind her closed, blindfolded eyes. The music built to a crescendo. She convulsed, her body overwrought with pleasure. Her mind numbed, drifting in a cloud of euphoria. Waves of release washed over her. Her senses mingled into one blissful existence. Subspace.

Alex roared, his body rigid as he fucked her through his orgasm. She curled her arms around his shoulders and held tightly to him. Sweat slicked his skin, and muscles bunched beneath her fingertips. Hard, pounding breaths strained his chest.

And then he took a long, replete exhale. The storm of release ebbed. He lowered onto her, letting her absorb the weight of his body. He kissed her and lifted the blindfold from her eyes.

She smiled. "Are you ready for today?" She combed her fingers through his hair.

Alex lifted his head. "Yes." He shifted back to his haunches and tugged the Velcro lose from her ankle straps.

She chuckled. "You're so cute." Pulling her knees in, she sat with her legs crossed at the top of the bed. "Really? Are you sure you want to do this?"

He crawled up the bed and nipped her lips. "You can show your family the ring on your finger or the one around your neck." He brushed a kiss to her lips. "But at some point, I'm going to have to meet them."

She touched the thin eternity collar circling the base of her throat. At first glance, the polished platinum choker might be considered expensive jewelry. Where an O-ring would dangle in the center, instead was the shape of a heart. And last night, he'd given her a ring — a two caret diamond engagement ring for the world to see. The gold band cut into her finger as she curled her left hand into a fist.

"Just remember me like this when you want to run the other way. My mother doesn't know how to mind her own business. Don't even hint at anything you don't want her neighbors to know about."

Alex shifted off the bed. "Noted."

"If you put on sports, and I use the term sport loosely. Football, golf, race car driving, even bowling, then you'll have my dad. If you have cheap beer, even better. He thinks microbrews and high-end beer all taste the same." She smiled. "I think my mom has killed his taste buds with her cooking. Which brings on another rule. If they offer dinner, can we insist on taking them out to eat? Unless you want to develop a taste for hamburger casserole, and even that is never the same thing twice."

Alex strode naked to the bathroom. Two dimples in his ass matched the one on his cheek.

"I still need to tell you about my sister, Jane."

"You forget, I already know about your family. I did my research."

She huffed. "You only know what's in my file."

"I'm taking a shower."

A moment passed as she waited to see how long it would take for him to start barking orders. He had a shower big enough for two, and he expected her to be in there with him.

"Now."

She giggled and slid off the bed.

I'm in love.

Before Alex, those words would have cut like a knife, slicing through her. But they didn't. Evelyn Larsen's heart pounded in ways she never expected. She wore her Dom's collar...and his ring. She was his weakness. He was her strength. When making love, sharing the same air, knowing she was the one giving him pleasure filled her, he completed her.

They belonged to each other. She wasn't damaged anymore. And neither was Alex. They were perfectly bound together...with leather and cuffs.

Dear Reader,
I hope you enjoyed Damaged - Initiation into Submission: High Protocol Book One
Alex and Evelyn will be a part of the High Protocol community. You'll see them in future books.

Next up is **Brutally Honest - Initiation into Submission: High Protocol Book Two.**
Misty's T-shirt says it all. Don't yuck someone's yum. Her yum? Judge and Kinbaku master Avery Lyons and his ropes.

The bonds of his rope…her initiation into submission.

Misty Kemp isn't submissive. She's fun, feisty, and isn't afraid to ask for what she wants. When asked to attend the City Gala, she trades her steel-toe work boots for garters and high heels…and meets the hot, newly elected Judge Avery Lyons.

Avery stepped away from the BDSM scene, giving up his rope when he put on the judge's robe. Since then, he's been hiding behind the bench, afraid of what discovery would do to his family and career. But Misty has his fingers itching to play. Getting involved is risky. She's not the kind of girl to be tied up, not even at the hands of a Kinbaku master.

She was supposed to be a one-night stand…or two. But he wants more and is willing to be brutally honest to prove it.

Then read **Forbidden - Initiation into Submission: High Protocol Book Three.** Get to know the elusive and naughty Dom of High Protocol – Ronan.

Saying his name…her initiation into submission.

Two things change a person—love and grief. Domestic violence councilor, Claire Orion shares both with her best friend Gavin. He's seen her at her darkest moments, held her through the storms of her life. She wants more, but he's kept a secret from her. In his world, he's called Ronan. He wants to hurt her, to chase the pain with pleasure.

High Protocol Manager, Gavin Sears has always loved sweet and innocent Claire. She is his island, a special place untouched by the BDSM world he lives in. He wants one touch, one taste, one time. But once will never be enough. When he gives in to forbidden desires, will she see her submission as beautiful…or abusive?

Beautiful Liar - Initiation into Submission: High Protocol Book Four

Dr. Brooks Leighton and Lyric Jones are magnets — drawn to each other. A sadist Dom and a masochist submissive can make beautiful music together.

The trust he earns...her initiation into submission.

Lyric Jones is a beautiful masochist. The scars across her body tell a dark and twisted tale. She aches for the pain of BDSM, but she lies to keep from being pulled back into the dangerous world she craves. She lies to hide her secrets. And she'll lie to protect the man who would make her his.

Dr. Brooks Leighton is immediately drawn to the submissive woman in his office. He's the match to her dark and tormented needs. If only she'll trust him with the secrets camouflaged in the butterflies and musical notes tattooed across her body. She is the music of his soul, but he'll drown in the silence of losing her unless he can show her she's safe in his arms.

Dangerously Bound - Initiation into Submission: High Protocol Book Five

Gabriella Ricci has a new bad boy boyfriend. Vance is determined to show her that she belongs on the back of his motorcycle…and chained to his bed.

The protection he gives her…her initiation into submission.

Gabriella Ricci is formidable in the office, but her personal life is a mess. Attractive men intimidate her and those she's trusted most have lied and betrayed her. When she meets a hot, tattooed bad boy, she takes a chance and climbs onto the back of his motorcycle. With Vance, she discovers a wild, reckless need for the BDSM pleasure promised in his bed.

Conformity was never a concern for Vance, until his high-risk lifestyle collided with responsibility. Now he's on the right side of the law. Although he's unapologetic in his pursuit of pleasure, his past carries a cost he's still paying. He'll never be good enough.

Insecurity runs deep within her, and Vance struggles with forgiveness. Are they opposites, destined to constantly push against each other? Or maybe they're less screwed up together.

Dangerously Bound begins the Heller Raiders MC romance series. Bad boy bikers, dangerous drama, and lots of steamy sex. These are gritty stories including violence, drug use and graphic language. Get ready for a wild ride.

Perfectly Played – Initiation into Submission: High Protocol Book Six

Tinker belongs to the dungeon. What happens when a dark and handsome Dom from an Italian crime family decides she's his?

The dangerous life he lives...her initiation into submission.

Tinker belongs to the BDSM dungeon. Pain and fear are part of the high of her submission. She wants more. She wants to be owned. But loyalties are tested when a powerful Dom with dangerous connections decides she's his.

Mafioso Luca Bruno is doing legitimate business with the owner of High Protocol. He desires more than a scene with the beautiful submissive. But he knows secrets that tie her to the underside of his crime family. Even if he is in bed with the enemy, no one takes what's his.

Mia and Luca are part of the upcoming Bruno Family Dark Mafia Romance Series. Look for Marco Bruno's story in 2023!

About the Author

KyAnn Waters is a multi-published, award-winning author of romance. She lives in Utah with her husband. Her two boys are grown and out in the world making mischief of their own. Never believing she was a pet lover, she still has made a home for a menagerie of animals. She enjoys sporting events on the television, thrillers on the big screen, and hot scenes between the pages of her books.

KyAnn loves to hear from readers. kyannwaters@hotmail.com

Visit her website www.KyAnnWaters.com

Books By KyAnn Waters

*After Dark
*All Lycan's Eve
*Beautiful Liar
*Beautiful Storm
*Bent For His Will
*Betrayed Vows
*Blade
*Born Into Fire
*Borrowing the Bride
*Brutally Honest
*Cinderella Undercover
*Damaged
*Dangerously Bound
*Dark Man: Blood Slaves Book 3
*Delicious Darkness
*Double Bang!
*Dozer
*Eternal Rapture
*Executive Positions
*Forbidden
*Going Down Hard
*Hard Ride Home
*Her Cowboy's Command
*Hot Blooded
*Ice Man: Blood Slaves Book 1
*Impulsive Pleasures
*Iron Man: Blood Slaves Book 2
*Johnny Loves Krissy

*Just Kiss Me
*Mercy of the Dragon
*Miranda's Rights
*Perfectly Played
*Private Lessons
*Rogue
*Romeo
*Roped and Branded
*Rough Justice
*Striker
*Syre
*Taking Command
*The Cougar Meets Her Master
*The Highlander's Improper Wife
*The Highlander's Unexpected Bride
*The Naughty List
*The Rented Bride
*Tie Me Up, Tie Me Down
*To Bed a Montana Man
*To Serve and Protect
*To Wed a Wanton Woman
*Twisted Sex and Happenstance
*Up Close and Personal
*Wanderlust
*Weekend Boyfriend
*With or Without You

Made in the USA
Middletown, DE
15 October 2023

40812425R00106